It was the first time a man had kissed her in three years.

It should have sent Carissa running straight for cover.

And he looked as shocked as she felt.

Swept off her feet.

This is magical. The words echoed through her head. The way his mouth had made her lips tingle. The Christmas tree lights and the scent of hot chocolate. The Christmassy music playing.

Yes, this was magical.

Unable to help herself, she reached up to lay the flat of her palm against his cheek.

"Quinn," she whispered, and he dipped his head again. Brushed his mouth against hers all over again. And she was shaking so much that she had to hold on to him to stop herself falling over on the ice. She felt as if she were spinning in an endless pirouette, faster and faster and totally out of control.

This had to stop.

And yet she didn't want it to stop.

Dear Reader,

I love Christmas. We celebrate it every single weekend in December (yes, with a full Christmas dinner), so we get to share it with my closest family and best friends—they live quite a way from us, so we don't get to see them on the day. I love the lights and the music, and doing silly Santa presents to open at the table after lunch, and planning surprises for Christmas stockings (my teenagers are not too old for this, and neither is my husband!). So Carissa has a lot in common with me.

So does her background—because the song that made her father famous is drawn from when my daughter's first Christmas was spent in hospital and my then 3-year-old son asked if Santa would bring his baby sister home for Christmas. (Yup, I wrote the song. The teens were a bit skeptical that playing the guitar counted as "research," but it did....)

But what if someone really hates Christmas? How can you persuade them to see the magic? That's what this book is about. Seeing the magic and learning to accept yourself for who you really are— so then you can be brave enough to give your whole heart.

I hope you enjoy Quinn and Carissa's story.

With love,

Kate Hardy

A New Year
Marriage Proposal
—

Kate Hardy

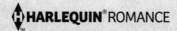
HARLEQUIN® ROMANCE

Recycling programs
for this product may
not exist in your area.

ISBN-13: 978-0-373-74315-5

A New Year Marriage Proposal

First North American Publication 2014

Copyright © 2014 by Pamela Brooks

Printed in U.S.A.

Kate Hardy lives in Norwich, in the east of England, with her husband, two young children, one bouncy spaniel and too many books to count! When she's not busy writing romance or researching local history she helps out at her children's schools. She also loves cooking—spot the recipes sneaked into her books! (They're also on her website, along with extracts and stories behind the books.) Writing for Harlequin has been a dream come true for Kate—something she's wanted to do ever since she was twelve. She also writes for the Harlequin® Medical Romance™ line.

Kate's always delighted to hear from readers, so do drop in to her website at www.katehardy.com.

Recent books by Kate Hardy:

CROWN PRINCE, PREGNANT BRIDE
BEHIND THE FILM STAR'S SMILE
BOUND BY A BABY
A DATE WITH THE ICE PRINCESS*
THE BROODING DOC'S REDEMPTION*
BALLROOM TO BRIDE AND GROOM
ONCE A PLAYBOY*

In Harlequin® Medical Romance™

This and other titles by Kate Hardy are also available in ebook format from www.Harlequin.com.

For Chris and Chloe—who inspired the song between them and who always make my Christmas special.

CHAPTER ONE

'GO AWAY,' QUINN O'NEILL muttered as the
doorbell rang. Right now was the worst possible time for an interruption; he was running
a test on the new system, and if it fell over
then he'd prefer to see it happen, to save him
having to wade through thousands of lines
of coding to find out exactly where the problem was. Whoever was at the door wasn't expected, hadn't been invited, and definitely
wasn't wanted right now. And who would ring
someone's doorbell at a quarter to eight in the
morning anyway?

The bell rang again.

Oh, for pity's sake. It wasn't as if he could
pause the test. If he cancelled it, that would
be an hour and a half wasted. 'Give up and go
away,' he said, scowling.

It rang again.

Whoever was at the front door clearly wasn't
going to go away, so he didn't really have any

choice. He'd have to answer the door, get rid of whoever it was as quickly as he could, and just hope that the system didn't fall over before he got back to it.

His first thought as he opened the door was that she looked like a lawyer or someone in high finance. She wore a little black suit—expensively cut—teamed with a crisp white shirt, soft burgundy leather gloves and a matching cashmere scarf as concessions to the chilly November morning, and killer high heels, with her blonde hair pulled back severely in a French pleat. Make-up that was barely there. Glasses that made her look academic and just a little bit intimidating. Lawyer, then.

'Yes?' he drawled.

She extended one hand, and he noticed then that she was carrying a large cylindrical tin and a plant as well as a briefcase. Leather. Expensive. Definitely something in law or the City.

'Mr O'Neill, welcome to Grove End Mews.' Her accent was totally plummy. Wealthy background, he guessed. Then again, given how much he'd just paid for his new house in Belgravia, it was pretty obvious that all his neighbours would be from wealthy backgrounds. Assuming she was his neighbour. But why else would she be welcoming him to the area?

As if his thoughts were written all over his face, she introduced herself. 'Carissa Wylde, chair of the residents' association.'

'Clarissa?'

'Carissa,' she corrected chirpily. 'No L.'

Clearly a lot of people made that mistake, then.

She gave him a sweet smile. 'I hope you've moved in OK. I brought you these from the Residents' Association to welcome you to the mews.'

Oh, no. He really didn't have time for this sort of nonsense. A residents' association was for busybodies with too much time on their hands, and he wanted no part of it. And wasn't that sort of thing normally chaired by someone on the far side of fifty, not someone who looked under thirty? 'It's very nice of you to call,' he said, not meaning a word of it, 'but I don't want to join any residents' association, thank you.' Before she could protest, he added, 'For the record, it doesn't worry me who parks where or what colour people want to paint their front doors. I'm not going to complain.'

'The Residents' Association isn't about that sort of thing.' Her smile didn't exactly falter, but it did become slightly more fixed. 'It's about mutual support and making life easier.'

For him, making life easier meant Carissa

Wylde going away and leaving him in peace. Preferably right now.

Before Quinn had the chance to say so, she added, 'So you know where to go if you need work done on your house, that sort of thing.'

He raised an eyebrow. 'You mean a cartel?'

'No,' she said crisply, 'but these are all listed houses, and the building regulations people are just a little bit picky about who they'll allow to work on them.'

'So why don't I just ask the building regulations people for a list if I need someone?'

'Because *my* list,' she said softly, 'comes with personal recommendations. So you know the contractors are child- and pet-friendly, clear up after themselves, do the job properly—and you're not going to get unwanted flashes of saggy bottoms.'

'Oh.' He felt slightly small.

'Welcome to Grove End Mews, Mr O'Neill,' she said again, then handed him the plant, the tin and an envelope that he guessed contained a 'welcome to your new home' card, then turned to go.

OK, she'd come at a bad time—but there was no way she could've known that. Most people would've assumed that he was busy unpacking and would welcome an interruption to give him a break, given that he'd moved in the day before. He glanced at the tin. It looked as if she'd brought him home-made cake. Still slightly warm, from the feel of the tin. She'd been kind. Welcomed him to the neighbourhood. And he'd just been really rude. Obnoxious, even. Not a good start. He raked his hand through his hair. 'Ms Wylde—wait.'

She turned back and looked at him. 'Yes?'

'Thank you for the plant. And the, um, cake.' At least, he assumed it was cake. Maybe she'd brought him cookies.

She shrugged. 'It's a tad more difficult to buy a welcome gift for a man. It's unlikely you'll even own a vase, so I thought a plant would be a safer bet than flowers—and by the way that's a dracaena, so you can get away with neglecting it a bit.'

Just as well. He didn't really do plants. He didn't do anything that needed looking after. Pets, plants and kids were all a total no-no in Quinn's world.

'Thank you,' he said again, feeling weirdly at a loss. How had she managed to do that?

'My pleasure.' The smile was back. 'See you later, Mr O'Neill.'

'Uh-huh.' He glanced at the front of the envelope. *Quinn O'Neill* was written in bold black script. He stared at her. 'How did you know my name?'

She shrugged. 'I have a good spy network.'

Obviously the surprise showed in his face because she tipped her head back and laughed. And Quinn was suddenly very aware of the curve of her throat. Pure, clean lines. And the temptation to lean over and touch his mouth to her throat heated his skin and shocked him in equal measure. He hadn't had such a physical reaction like that to anyone for longer than he could remember.

'I was friends with Maddie and Jack, who lived here before you,' she explained. 'They told me your name.'

'Of course.' He rolled his eyes. 'I should have worked that out for myself.' Spy network, indeed. Of course that hadn't been a crack about what he did for a living. Because she wouldn't have a clue what he did…would she?

'Moving house is one of the most stressful life events and I've obviously caught you at a bad moment. I'm sorry. I'll let you get on,' she said. 'I'm at number seven if you need anything or want an introduction to people.'

Again, she gave him one of those sweet smiles, and Quinn was stunned to realise that it had completely scrambled his brains, because all he could manage in reply was, 'Uh-huh.' And then he watched her walk swiftly down the paved street outside the mews, her heels clicking on the stone slabs. The way her bottom swayed as she walked put him in a daze.

What the hell was wrong with him?

He never let himself get distracted from his work. Well, except for when he'd dated Tabitha, and he'd been twenty-one and naïve back then. He hadn't been enough for her—and he'd vowed then not to repeat that mistake and to keep his heart intact in future. He knew it had given him a reputation of being a bit choosy and not letting people close—but it was easier that way. And he made it clear from the outset that his relationships were fun and strictly short term, so nobody got hurt.

So why, now, was he letting a complete stranger distract him?

'Get real. Even if she's single—and, looking like that, I doubt it very much—you are most definitely not getting involved. You just don't have time for this,' he told himself sharply, closed the door and headed back to his computer. And hoped the system hadn't fallen over…

Carissa was already at her desk at Hinchcliffe and Turnbull by the time her PA walked in with a large mug of coffee, made just the way

Carissa liked it. Carissa looked up and smiled. 'Morning, Mindy.'

'Sorry I'm late. The bus got held up,' Mindy said. 'I'll stay late tonight to make up the time.'

Carissa smiled and shook her head. 'No, it's fine. Don't worry about it. You're almost never late, and you work through your lunch break when you shouldn't as it is. Thanks for the coffee.'

'Thank *you* for the brownies,' Mindy said, referring to the parcel that Carissa had left on her desk. 'Have I told you lately that you're the best boss in the world?'

Carissa laughed. 'Don't let Sara hear you say that. We're supposed to be the joint best, given that we job-share.'

'Sara doesn't make me cake,' Mindy said. 'But OK, I won't tell her. Your ten o'clock appointment just phoned to say he's running fifteen minutes late, so I'll ring your eleven o'clock to see if he can wait a little.'

'Great,' Carissa said. 'If not, then I'll try and wrap up the ten o'clock as near on time as I can, if you can stall Mr Eleven o'Clock for a few minutes with some of your fantastic coffee.'

'But not with the brownies,' Mindy said, laughing as she headed for the door. 'Because they're mine—all mine!'

Carissa leaned back in her chair and sipped her coffee. Weird how she couldn't concentrate today. Normally by now she'd have lists written and she'd be knee-deep in something to do with contract law. But today her mind kept returning to her new neighbour.

Quinn O'Neill.

Maddie hadn't known much about him, other than his name and the fact he was single. She thought he might be something to do with computers. Something very well paid, if he could afford a three-bedroom house in Grove End Mews.

Yet Quinn definitely didn't look like the kind of man who wore a suit and tie to the office. This morning he'd been wearing faded jeans, a T-shirt that was equally faded with half the print of the band's logo worn away, and canvas shoes without socks.

Not that you'd wear your best clothes when you were unpacking boxes, but even so. There was something that didn't quite add up. Scruffiness didn't tend to go with the kind of money you needed to buy a mews house in Belgravia. The rest of her male neighbours were all clean-shaven and had immaculate hair. Quinn O'Neill had had two-day-old stubble and hair that made him look as if he'd just got out of bed.

And she wished she hadn't thought about that. Because now she was imagining him just climbing out of her bed. Naked. Wearing only that stubble and a very wicked smile.

What on earth was she doing? She knew better than that. Since Justin, she'd avoided all relationships, not trusting herself to get it right next time and pick one of the good guys. Why on earth was she indulging in ridiculous fantasies about a man she'd only just met and knew practically nothing about? A man, furthermore, who'd made it very clear that he wasn't interested in overtures of friendship from anyone in Grove End Mews and wanted to be left alone?

She managed to concentrate on her file for the next ten minutes.

But then Quinn O'Neill's face was back in her mind's eye. Dark eyes lit with mischief. A mouth promising rich rewards for giving in to temptation. And hair that looked as if it had just been mussed by a lover.

Oh, for pity's sake. Why couldn't she get him out of her head?

She needed a reality check. Like now. To stop her making the same mistakes all over again. Yes, her instincts were to trust him; but then again her instincts had been wrong when it had come to Justin. What was to say that she'd learned her lesson? It wasn't a risk she wanted to take.

She pulled her computer keyboard towards her, flicked into the internet, and typed his name into the search engine.

The most interesting page was a fairly recent one from the *Celebrity Life!* website. Carissa didn't usually read gossip magazines, not enjoying their exaggeration and the speculation with a slightly nasty edge; but the headline had grabbed her attention: 'Smart Is the New Sexy.'

According to the article, Quinn was a real-life 'Q', developing gadgets and computer systems for the government.

Which suddenly made him a lot more interesting to Carissa. He might just turn out to be the missing piece she needed. Not just for the extra-special Santa she was planning for the ward opening next month, but for several other projects as well. That would put him very safely on the not-mixing-business-with-pleasure list, so she could think about him strictly in terms of business in future and not let herself wonder what his mouth would feel like against hers.

And if he was freelance—as the article hinted—then he might be open to persuasion to help her.

But what would persuade Quinn O'Neill to work on Project Sparkle?

She could afford to pay him the going rate, but she wanted people on her team who cared about more than just money or status. Particularly as Project Sparkle was something that she tried to keep out of the media. She needed someone with a good heart.

Did Quinn O'Neill have a good heart?

The article couldn't tell her that. And, actually, it didn't say that much about what he did in his job; the journalist hinted that it was forbidden by the Official Secrets Act. But maybe Quinn was just a little bit vain, because after all he *had* posed for photographs. In some of them, he was wearing a very expensively cut suit, a crisp white shirt and an understated silk tie. More James Bond than Sherlock Holmes, she thought; but if Quinn was good at solving problems then the headline did perhaps have a point.

'Mindy,' Carissa asked, when her PA came in with the post, 'would you agree with this headline?'

Mindy took the magazine and studied the pages. 'Yum,' she said. 'Yes.' Then she looked at Carissa. 'Why?'

'No reason,' Carissa said. 'Just idle curiosity.'

'I've worked with you for five years,' Mindy reminded her. 'You haven't dated for the last three. For you to ask me if I think a guy is sexy means—'

'I don't date because I'm busy with my work,' Carissa cut in.

They both knew that wasn't the real reason Carissa didn't date. And they both knew that Carissa would absolutely not discuss it. Mindy was one of the three people who knew exactly what scars Justin had left—and the subject was permanently closed.

'He's asked you out?' Mindy asked.

'That's ridiculous. No. He's moved in, three doors down,' Carissa responded. 'I was thinking, I could use some of his skills.'

Mindy skimmed through the article and raised her eyebrows. 'For Project Sparkle, you mean?' she asked, lowering her voice.

'And for the opening of the Wylde Ward. But I need an idea of what might persuade him to help me. Besides money, obviously.'

'Make him some of your brownies,' Mindy said promptly. 'Give them to him when they're just out of the oven.'

'I already did that, this morning,' Carissa said. 'As a moving-in present.'

'Bad, *bad* idea.' Mindy rolled her eyes. 'You should have given him a shop-bought cake if you really had to give the guy some cake. Your brownies are special, and not to be wasted. They're your secret weapon—and you don't use your secret weapon on day one. You wait until the appropriate time to use it.'

Carissa couldn't help laughing. 'He might not even like chocolate.'

'Then that would make him totally wrong for Project Sparkle in any case,' Mindy retorted.

'I guess.' Carissa shook herself. 'Right. To work. And thanks, Mindy.'

'Any time. Oh, and your eleven o'clock agreed to move his slot back by fifteen minutes. You're good to go.'

'You,' Carissa said, 'are wonderful.'

'Just keep bringing the brownies,' Mindy said with a grin.

When Quinn's stomach rumbled, he remembered that he hadn't actually had time for breakfast yet. He couldn't be bothered to go down to the kitchen to grab some cereal but he did have the tin of cake that Carissa Wylde had given him.

And there was nobody there to complain that cake wasn't a breakfast food. Nobody to count the carbs and sigh and look pained. Nobody to stop him doing what he wanted because her needs had to come first, second and third.

He opened the tin.

The cake smelled good. Really good.

He picked up a square. Still warm, too. Crisp edges against his fingertips, and yet there was enough give when he held it for him to know that the inside would be deliciously squidgy.

He took a bite.

Heaven in a cube.

Had Carissa made the brownies herself? If so, he was going to find out what he could trade her for more of those brownies, fresh out of the oven. Maybe she had a temperamental laptop that needed coaxing back to life every so often. Something that wouldn't take him long to fix—just long enough for her to be grateful and make him some brownies. He made a mental note to float that one by her, and then finished off the rest of the tin.

The brownies kept him going all day, until he'd finished the testing and was satisfied that the system did exactly what he'd designed it to do. A quick call to let his client know that all was well and he'd install everything at their office first thing tomorrow, and he was done.

Which left unpacking.

Not that he had huge amounts of boxes. He kept as much as he could digitally. Lots of clutter meant lots of dust. And he'd never seen the point in the knick-knacks his aunt displayed on her mantelpiece and in her china cabinet. If it wasn't functional, Quinn wasn't interested. Minimalism suited him much better.

He'd already done the important stuff yesterday—his office and his bed. The rest of it could wait.

He glanced at his watch.

Half past seven.

Was it too late to call in at number seven and return the cake tin to Carissa Wylde? Or would she be in the middle of dinner?

There was only one way to find out. Either way, he could talk to her or arrange a time to talk to her.

And this had nothing at all to do with the fact that every time he'd looked away from his computer desk that day he'd seen her laughing in his mind's eye, the curve of her throat soft and tempting and inviting.

He washed up the tin, dried it, and walked out into the mews to ring Carissa's doorbell. She answered the door in less than a minute— still dressed in this morning's black suit and white shirt, though this time she'd changed the killer heels. For bunny slippers. Which should've made him sneer, but actually it made her endearingly cute.

'Oh. Mr O'Neill.'

Given that he'd been a bit gruff with her this morning, it wasn't surprising that she looked a bit wary of him now. 'Quinn,' he said, hoping that the offer of first-name terms was enough of an overture. 'I'm returning your tin. Thank you for the cake.'

'Pleasure. I hope you liked it.'

'I did. I liked it a lot,' he said, and her cheeks went pink with pleasure.

Which was bad, because now he was imagining her face flushed for quite a different reason. For goodness' sake. Could his libido not keep itself under control for two minutes? And he really didn't think that a woman like Carissa Wylde would agree to the terms he insisted on nowadays when it came to relationships—light, a bit of fun, and absolute emotional distance. Nothing serious. Nothing deep. Nothing that could end up with him getting hurt. His instincts told him that she was the sort who'd want closeness. Something that wasn't in his skill set. Which would mean she'd get hurt—and he didn't want to hurt her.

'Would you like a cup of tea?' she asked.

How terribly English and upper class she sounded, he thought, faintly amused—and yet she was more than a stereotype. She drew him. Intrigued him. And a cup of tea wouldn't hurt, would it? It didn't mean getting close. It meant being neighbourly.

'That would be nice,' he said. 'If your husband doesn't mind.'

Her face shuttered. 'No husband. And, even if there was one, I have the right to invite a neighbour in for a cup of tea.'

Ouch. He'd clearly trodden on a sore spot. 'Sorry. I didn't mean to…' Hmm. She was clearly a rich, successful businesswoman. Maybe a divorced one. And he didn't have ridiculous preconceptions about a woman's place in any case. 'I didn't mean to imply,' he said, 'that you needed a husband to validate you.'

She looked surprised, then pleased. 'Apology accepted. Come in.'

And how different her house was from his own. The air smelled of beeswax—clearly any wood in the house was polished to within an inch of its life—and the lights were soft and welcoming rather than stark and functional. He noted fresh flowers in the hallway. And he'd just bet that her living room held cases of leather-bound books. Carissa looked like a woman who read rather than flicking endlessly through channels of repeats on satellite TV.

When she led him through to the kitchen, he wasn't surprised to see that the work surfaces weren't covered in clutter. But it was definitely a kitchen that was used rather than one that was all for show. An efficient one, he thought, tallying with his view of her as a successful businesswoman.

She used proper tea leaves rather than teabags—so clearly she had an eye for detail and liked things done properly—and her teapot was silver. Quinn had a nasty feeling that it was solid silver rather than silver plate. As was the tea strainer. And the sugar bowl and spoons.

Old money, then? Very different from his own background. Not that it mattered. He'd made his own way in life, and he was comfortable with who he was.

'Milk?' she asked.

'Please.'

And she proceeded to pour him the perfect cup of tea. In what looked like an antique porcelain cup.

It was made even more perfect by the fact that she'd placed more brownies on a matching porcelain plate.

'Help yourself,' she said.

'Thank you.' He didn't need a second invitation.

'So, Mr O'Neill. Quinn.' She smiled at him. 'The real-life Q.'

He almost choked on his brownie. Particularly when she added, '"Smart Is the New Sexy."'

He groaned, knowing exactly what she was referring to. 'Just ignore anything you read in that magazine. Please,' he added, looking pained. 'I only did the interview as a favour to a friend, and her boss went a bit mad with it. I didn't say half of what was reported. And I'm not...' Time to shut up. Before he dug that hole any deeper.

'The looks bit I can judge for myself,' she said, and a prickle of awareness ran up his spine.

He was definitely attracted to her.

Was she saying that she was attracted to him?

She had no husband. He had no wife.

There was no reason why they couldn't...

Apart from the fact that he didn't do closeness. And he had a feeling that would be a deal-breaker for her.

'The rest of it...is it true?' she asked. 'You develop gadgets?'

'A lot of what I do,' he said carefully, 'is bound by the Official Secrets Act.'

'So basically, if you tell me what you really do, you'll have to kill me.'

She was so irrepressible that he couldn't help smiling. 'Yes.'

'Good. So you can keep things confidential.'

Where was this going? he wondered, but inclined his head.

'Strong and silent.' She took a sip of her tea. 'But what I really want to know is if you can build systems.'

'What kind of systems?'

'Computer systems. Clever ones.' She looked him straight in the eye. 'At ridiculously short notice.'

Yes, yes and yes. 'Why?'

'Because, Mr O'Neill, I have a proposition for you.'

He had a sudden vision of her in a pretty dress with her hair loose, laughing up at him and offering a kiss...

No. If he had any kind of relationship at all with Carissa Wylde, it would be very simple, very defined, and with built-in barriers. Neighbours or strictly business. Nothing closer. 'A business proposition,' he clarified.

'Of course.'

Which should be a relief. But instead it tied him up in knots, which he really hadn't expected. He didn't *want* to get involved with anyone. He liked his life the way it was.

But clearly his mouth wasn't listening to his head, because he found himself saying, 'Tell me more.'

CHAPTER TWO

'I WANT YOU to build me a virtual Santa,' Carissa said. 'It's for the opening of a new children's ward.'

'A virtual Santa.' Now Quinn understood: obviously she worked in PR. That would explain the expensive clothes—and the glasses. To make her look serious rather than fluffy. Image was everything in PR. And the fact that she could even consider commissioning something without having to ask the price first meant that she didn't have to defer to anyone on her budget; so she was the owner or director of the company and the client trusted her judgement absolutely. 'Why can't you have a real Santa?'

'I intend to,' she said. 'But I need the virtual one first.'

'Why? Surely a real Santa would come with a sack of gifts?'

A tiny pleat appeared between her eyebrows. 'He will. But the virtual one will chat to them first. A life-sized one—I guess a holographic thing will probably be too difficult to do at short notice, but we could have a life-sized screen. Santa will get them to say what they really want for Christmas. In the meantime, people behind the scenes can buy the gifts, wrap them and label them, and then the real Santa walks in with all the gifts on his sleigh, and he delivers their perfect Christmas present.'

Quinn could see exactly how the system could work. It wouldn't take very much effort at all to build the system she wanted. And suddenly everything was all right again: he could treat this as a business project.

'OK. Does it have to be life-sized? Because a screen that big is going to be really costly,' he warned. She might be able to persuade various businesses to donate or loan some equipment, but not for something as specialised as that.

She thought about it. 'Some of the children might be too sick to leave their beds. I guess something portable would be better for them— so basically we're taking Santa to them. And if everyone uses the same system then nobody will feel left out or different.'

'So you could use a laptop or tablet, say.' He thought about it. 'That'd be very doable.

And it would save you money if you could use something you already have.'

'And I was thinking maybe we could use the barcodes on an appointment letter or the children's medical notes, so Santa knows the children's names even as they look at the screen,' she said.

He shook his head. 'No chance. You'll fall foul of all the data protection laws. You'd have to get permission from the health authority to use their data—and, believe me, you'd have to jump through hoops to get that permission—and then you'd also need written permission from every single parent or guardian. It's not going to happen. You need a different way of doing it.'

'So what would you suggest?' she asked.

'Give me until tomorrow to think about it,' he said, 'and I'll come up with a plan. How are you organising the gifts?'

'Santa will pass the information to a team who'll source the gifts, buy them, get them wrapped and couriered over to the hospital. Timing's going to be a bit tight, but it's doable,' she said. 'Don't worry about that bit. I've already got an arrangement with a couple of large toy shops and department stores.'

'They're donating the gifts?'

'No. We're picking up the costs. They've

just agreed to supply what we want and give us priority treatment.'

Quinn had the distinct feeling that this was personal as well as business. Maybe Carissa knew a child who'd been in hospital at Christmas. Someone who'd been close to her.

'It's the virtual Santa that's important,' she added.

'And you have someone lined up to play him?'

'I do,' she said. 'One last thing.'

'Yes?'

There was a hint of anxiety in her eyes. 'This has to be totally confidential.'

He didn't get it. 'Isn't the whole point of PR to get media coverage?'

'For the opening of the children's ward, yes. For the person behind Santa, no.'

Maybe it wasn't personal for her, then. Maybe it was personal for her client—and Carissa was the kind of PR professional who'd go the extra mile to make sure that her clients got exactly what they wanted.

'Got it. OK. Let's have an update meeting tomorrow at my place,' he said. 'I'll give you timings, costs and a workable solution.'

'That,' she said, 'sounds perfect.'

'What time do you want to meet?'

'Seven?' she suggested. 'If that works for you.'

'It works.' He finished his tea and stood up. 'Thank you for the tea and brownies, Ms Wylde.'

'Carissa,' she corrected. 'Thank you for taking on the project. I'll make sure your invoice is processed promptly.'

'You haven't asked my hourly rate yet,' he said.

'I'm sure it will be in line with the market rate.'

Meaning that she'd make him feel guilty and he'd cut his rate if it was too high. He was about to agree, but his mouth went freelance on him again. 'Make me some more of that cake and we'll call tonight's meeting a freebie.'

'Deal,' she said.

And when he shook her hand, his palm actually tingled.

Not good.

This was business. And she was his neighbour. And you most definitely didn't mix any of those things with anything else, not if you wanted a quiet life where you could just get on with your work without your heart being tied up in knots all the time.

'Tomorrow,' he said, and left before he did anything stupid. Like turning her hand over and kissing her wrist. Letting his mouth linger on her pulse point. And asking her for a date.

What Carissa had learned about Quinn O'Neill: he was bright. He liked chocolate. He had a good heart. And he was *definitely* smart as well as sexy.

But she'd just involved him in the project she'd been working on for years. Something she couldn't afford to go wrong, because it was way too important to her. In her experience, getting involved meant getting out of her depth. Getting hurt. She'd only just managed to paper over the cracks post-Justin; the glue still needed time to dry, time to help her form a shell to keep her heart safe. So having any kind of involvement with Quinn other than a business relationship—even if he was smart, sexy and sensitive—would be a very bad idea.

'He's off limits,' she told herself. Out loud, just to make sure she'd got the message.

But she still couldn't quite get him out of her head.

She worked through her lunch hour the next day so she'd be home in time to make brownies before the meeting. And at precisely seven she rang Quinn's doorbell.

'Punctual. Good. Come in.' He glanced at the cake tin. 'Last night's fee?'

'Last night's fee,' she confirmed.

'Good. Thank you.' He took the tin from her. 'Coffee?'

'Thanks. Milk, no sugar,' she said.

'Come up.'

The layout of Quinn's house was very similar to her own; she remembered it from visiting Maddie and Jack. Like her, he had a table in the kitchen where he could eat—or work maybe. He gestured to her to sit down, and switched on the kettle.

Like her, she noticed, he had no clutter on the worktops. But it didn't feel like a cook's kitchen. Though maybe she was being unfair. He'd only moved in two days before. He'd barely had time to unpack—and she'd noticed a few cardboard boxes by the door to the living room. It made her flush with guilt; he'd hardly even moved in, and she'd already inveigled him into working extra hours on her project, fitting it around whatever work he already had on, knowing that freelancers rarely said no because they couldn't afford to pass up a project in case it left them with a gap in their schedule—and their finances.

Before she could apologise for being pushy, Quinn put a mug of coffee in front of her. He opened the lid of the cake tin but didn't put the brownies on a plate. 'Help yourself,' he said.

'Right. I've been thinking about how your system could work.'

Guilt flooded over her. 'I'm sorry for dumping extra work on you,' she said in a rush.

He scoffed. 'What you wanted isn't rocket science. Well, it might've been if you'd insisted on a life-size virtual Santa. This is easy and it took me about five minutes to work it all out. What you need is a simple video link. We'll avoid microphone noise by getting Santa to wear a wire—and the person at the children's ward who takes the tablet round to the kids also needs to wear a wire.'

'That would be me. And they're going to see if I'm wearing a microphone or headset. I guess you can hide Santa's in his hat or beard, but…' She grimaced. 'I don't want them to see mine.'

'They're not going to see anything,' he said. 'When I say wearing a wire, I don't mean a physical wire—it's not like the kind of thing you saw on cop shows twenty years ago, where someone had a microphone taped to his chest and attached to a recording device worn round his waist. I mean having an app on the tablet and doing the "wire" through software. The audio quality's better than an old-fashioned wire or a headset.'

She blinked. 'You can do that?'

'It's not new technology,' he informed her. 'And it's not as if we need to miniaturise anything or hide it in something tiny in a way that means it'll get past any detection equipment.'

Which sounded as if he did that sort of thing all the time.

'You're carrying a tablet so the kids can see Santa and talk to him. The app runs unobtrusively in the background.'

'I feel a bit stupid,' she admitted.

'Unless you work in the area, how are you meant to know the technology exists?' he asked.

Carissa mentally added 'kind' to Quinn's list of attributes. And tried very hard not to think about 'Smart Is the New Sexy'. Justin had been sexy, too. Smart. And he'd been the biggest mistake of her life. She couldn't risk getting things wrong like that again.

'So. The app broadcasts the audio—not just to Santa, but through headphones to the support team. You tell us the patient's name just before you take the tablet over to the child, so Santa can get the name right and do the "magic" bit by greeting the kid by name.

'The team picks up what the child wants as a gift and organises it with your supplier on another line—they'll be able to hear you clearly, but you won't be able to hear anyone except

Santa on the tablet. And your team will work on collaborative software with a database so they all know who's ordered what and from where—that way, nothing gets missed or duplicated.'

'And you have this collaborative software?' she asked.

'Yes, and I can tweak it to suit your needs. I can train your team on it so they'll be perfect within about half an hour.'

She looked at him. 'I don't know what to say. Except I'm impressed.'

'It's really not rocket science,' he said again. 'It's just putting a couple of systems together.'

'Have you actually worked in rocket science, then?' The question came out before she could stop it.

Quinn wrinkled his nose, and Carissa had to tell herself not to notice how cute it made him look. 'I can't answer that,' he said.

She blew out a breath. 'OK. Timings and costings?'

'When's the opening day?'

'Four weeks tomorrow.' The anniversary of her parents' plane crash. So she'd have something good to look forward to on that day, to take the sting out of it. And it had felt fitting to do something in their memory on that day.

'You can have the software to play with at

any time in the next week. And I'll give you
the paperwork tomorrow.' He paused. 'Do you
need virtual reindeer?'

'No. I have real ones.'

'OK. Then we're done.' He paused. 'Unless
you want to stay for dinner.'

Dinner with Quinn O'Neill.

Of course he didn't mean candlelight, roses
and vintage champagne. Or somewhere under
the stars on a roof garden. Particularly in November. Just why were these ridiculous ideas
seeping into her head? The man was a neighbour. A work colleague, of sorts. Not a potential date. And she didn't do dates anyway.
This was a business meeting and it was about
the time that most people ate in the evening.
They both had to eat, so they might as well
eat together. It didn't mean anything deeper
than that.

He was waving a piece of paper at her. A
menu.

'Takeaway pizza?' she asked.

'Works for me.'

Now she had a better idea why his kitchen
hadn't had a cook's vibe about it. She'd just
bet his fridge was bare, too, except for milk
and maybe some cheese. She had a feeling that
Quinn O'Neill was the kind of man who forgot
to eat when he was busy, or lived on takeaway

food and didn't notice what he was eating—it was fuel, and nothing more than that.

'Pizza,' she said.

He gave her a pointed look. 'Don't tell me you don't eat carbs. Not when you make brownies as good as those.'

'No. Of course I eat carbs. But…takeaway pizza. The stuff with a thick crust. Ick.' She liked the thin, crispy type. She grimaced and shook her head. 'Look, I have fresh tuna and some stir-fry veg in my fridge. Why don't we have dinner at mine?'

'Healthy food. Fish and vegetables.' He looked slightly disgusted.

She hid a smile. Just as she'd thought: he lived on junk. She could offer a compromise there. 'And polenta fries.'

He looked thoughtful. 'Are they as good as your brownies?'

'According to my best friend, yes.'

'Done,' he said. 'I'll bring wine.'

'Are you quite sure you don't want a wheat-grass shot?'

'I'm going to pretend,' he said, 'that you're teasing, because I have a nasty feeling you might actually be serious—and there's no way I'm drinking a glass of green gloop.'

'I was teasing. Though I could source it.'

He grimaced and shook his head. 'No need. How long does it take to make polenta fries?'

'About forty minutes.'

'Which gives me time to go and find some wine.'

Of course he wouldn't have wine, especially if his fridge was practically bare. Plus he'd only just moved in. 'You really don't have to bring wine,' she said.

'I do. And pudding,' he said. 'Because you're not getting these brownies back. This is business, so we'll both bring something to the table.'

Business. She was glad he'd said that. Because it stopped her fantasising about something truly stupid. Such as what it would be like to have a proper date with Quinn O'Neill. She wasn't ready for dating again. She wasn't sure if she'd ever be ready. But business she could do.

'OK. Deal. See you in thirty minutes or so,' she said.

Quinn hit pure gold in the wine shop: they had a deli section, with a display of French *macarons* in pretty colours.

Pistachio, vanilla, coffee. And then some more unusual flavours: violet and blueberry, white chocolate and pomegranate, crème brûlée, salted caramel. The perfect gift for a foodie like Carissa, he thought.

He bought a boxful, plus a bottle of flinty Chablis.

Back at the mews, he rang Carissa's doorbell.

She answered the door wearing a cotton apron covered in hearts over her skirt and shirt; it made her look younger and much more approachable than she'd seemed the first time he'd met her.

'Hi,' she said. 'Dinner's almost ready.'

He handed her the bottle and the box. 'The box needs to go in the fridge,' he said. 'The wine's already chilled.'

'Thank you—though you really didn't need to bring anything. Come up.'

He closed the door behind them and followed her up the stairs to her kitchen. She'd laid her kitchen table, he noticed, with a white damask tablecloth, solid silver cutlery, very elegant fine glassware and a white porcelain vase containing deep purple spray carnations.

'Is there anything I can do to help?' he asked.

'Given that you waved a pizza menu at me, can you actually cook?' she teased.

'I make great toasted sandwiches, I'll have you know,' he protested.

She just laughed, and again he had a vision of the way she'd laughed on his doorstep, tipping her head back.

Down, boy, he told his libido sharply.

All the same, he couldn't take his eyes off her as she stood by the hob, stirring vegetables in a wok. Did she have the faintest clue how gorgeous she was?

The radio was playing a song he really loathed: 'Santa, Bring My Baby Home for Christmas.' A super-sweet Christmas song that always meant the festive season was on its way. Quinn's least favourite time of year. Funny, he'd expected Carissa to listen to opera or highbrow stuff, not a singalong pop station. Which just went to show that you shouldn't assume things about people.

'That song's so terrible,' he said, rolling his eyes. 'Talk about cheesy. And sugary.'

'Rather a mix of metaphors,' she said drily.

'You know what I mean.' He sang along with the chorus. '"I wish, my baby, you were home tonight; I wish, my baby, I could hold you tight. Santa, bring my baby home for Christmas; Santa, bring my baby home to me."' He grimaced. 'It's terrible!'

'Well, hey.' She spread her hands. 'Meet the original baby.'

'What?' He wasn't following this conversation. At all. Or was she teasing him, the way she had about the wheatgrass shot? Did she just have a weird sense of humour?

'My dad wrote that song,' she said. 'About me.'

He blinked. 'Your dad?'

'Uh-huh. Pete Wylde. The Wylde Boys,' she expanded.

He was silenced momentarily. Carissa Wylde was the daughter of the late musician Pete Wylde. And Quinn hadn't made the connection. At all.

'I'm sorry,' he said. 'I…um…'

'You hate Dad's music.' She shrugged. 'Each to their own taste.'

'No, I do like some of his stuff. Just not the Christmas song. And I'm digging myself a deeper hole here.' He blew out a breath. 'I really don't mean to insult you, Carissa.'

'It's OK. I won't hold it against you.'

Her voice was neutral and her face was impassive, and he didn't have a clue what she was thinking. 'So your father actually wrote the song for you?'

'My first Christmas,' she said. 'I was only a few weeks old. I was in hospital for a week with a virus that meant I couldn't breathe very easily, and I had to be fed by a tube until I was better. The only way Dad coped with it was to bring his guitar to the hospital, sit by my bed and play me songs. That's why he wrote "Santa, Bring My Baby Home for Christmas".'

And now Quinn understood for the first time what the song was actually saying. Pete Wylde had wanted his tiny baby daughter home for her first Christmas, safe and well and in his arms. It wasn't a cheesy love song at all. It had come straight from the heart.

'I'm sorry,' he said again. And not just because he'd insulted her. Because he was envious. What would it be liked to be loved and wanted so much by your family? It was something he'd never had. His mother had been quick enough to dump him on his aunt and uncle, and he'd always felt a bit like a spare part in their home. Which was probably why he was antsy about getting attached to anyone now: it was something he'd never really done.

'You don't need to like the song,' she said with a smile. 'Though plenty of people do. It makes shedloads of royalties every Christmas.'

But Quinn was pretty sure that money wasn't what motivated Carissa Wylde. 'And?'

'Dad arranged to put half the royalties from the song in a trust,' she said. 'Which has been enough to fund the building and equipping of a new children's ward, including an intensive

care unit. All state-of-the-art equipment—and
we'll be able to keep it that way in the future.'

'The ward that needs a virtual Santa.' It
dawned on him now. '*You're* the client.'

'Uh-huh.'

'So do you do PR for anyone else?'

She frowned. 'PR?'

'That's what you do, isn't it? PR?'

'No. I'm a lawyer,' she said.

So he'd been right first time round. 'Oh.'

'Sit down,' she said, 'or if you want you can
grab the corkscrew from the drawer and open
that lovely wine you brought. Third drawer on
the right.'

She was letting him off the hook. And he
was grateful. 'Thank you.' He opened the wine
while she served up the tuna and the vegetables. Porcelain flatware, he noticed, and she
served the vegetables in dishes rather than just
sharing them out onto their plates. Carissa
Wylde did things formally. Completely the opposite of how he did things, outside work. He
was quite happy to eat pizza straight out of the
box or Chinese food straight from the carton.

'Well.' She stripped off the apron, folded it
and placed it on the worktop, no doubt ready to
be transferred to the washing machine. Then
she sat down opposite him and lifted her glass

in a toast. 'Here's to the opening of the Wylde Ward and our virtual Santa.'

'The opening of the Wylde Ward and the virtual Santa,' he echoed, and smiled at her. 'It's nice that it's named after your dad.'

'And my mum,' she pointed out.

'That's nice,' he said again, feeling horrendously awkward and not quite sure how to deal with this. Things had suddenly become a lot more complicated.

'Help yourself before it gets cold.' She indicated the food.

What he'd thought would be plain vegetables had clearly been cooked with a spice mix. A gorgeous one. And the polenta fries were to die for. 'If you ever get bored with being a lawyer,' he said, 'I think you'd make a good chef.'

'Cook,' she corrected. 'Maybe.'

'Didn't you ever think about being a musician? I mean, given what your dad did?'

She shook her head. 'I can play the piano a bit, but I don't have that extra spark that Dad had. And life as a musician isn't an easy one. In the early days, he and Mum lived pretty much hand to mouth. He was so lucky that the right break came at the right time.' She paused. 'What about you? Do you come from a long line of inventors?'

Quinn didn't have a clue who his father was.

And the family he'd been dumped on…well. He'd just been a burden to them. The unwanted nephew. One who definitely hadn't planned to spend his career working in their corner shop, which in turn had made him even more unwanted. 'No.'

He'd sounded shorter than he'd meant to, because it killed the conversation dead. She just ate her tuna steak and looked faintly awkward.

In the end, he sighed. 'Why is it I constantly feel the need to apologise around you?'

'Because you're being a grumpy idiot?' she suggested.

'You don't pull your punches, do you?' he asked wryly. 'I hope I never end up in court in front of you.'

'I'm a solicitor, not a barrister,' she said. 'Gramps's chambers would've taken me on as a pupil but…' she pulled a face '…I didn't really want to do all the performance stuff. Wearing the robes and the wig, doing all the flashy rhetoric and showing off in front of a jury. I prefer the backroom stuff—working with the law, with words and people.'

'So it's in the family? Being a lawyer?'

'On my mum's side, yes. I think Gramps was a bit disappointed that she never became a lawyer, but she met Dad at a gig when she was a student, fell in love with him, and then

I came along.' She smiled. 'Though I think Gramps was quite pleased when he realised I was more likely to follow in his footsteps than in Dad's.'

Quinn had had nobody's footsteps to follow in. He'd made his own way. 'I guess that made it easier for you.'

'More like it meant I had something to live up to,' she corrected.

He'd never thought of it that way before— that privilege could also be a burden. Tabitha's friends and family had all been privileged, and they'd taken their easy life for granted; they'd also looked down on those who'd had to work for what they had, like him. Clearly Clarissa saw things very differently.

'I had to be the best, because I couldn't let Gramps down,' she continued. 'If I fell flat on my face, it wouldn't just be me that looked an idiot. No way would I do that to him. I wanted him to be proud of me, not embarrassed by my incompetence.'

Quinn hadn't known Carissa for very long, but incompetence was a word he'd never associate with her. And he'd just bet that her grandparents adored her as much as her parents obviously had, because her voice was full of affection rather than fear or faint dislike. 'Do your grandparents know what you're doing about the ward?'

'The ward itself, yes, of course—Gramps was really good at helping me cut through the red tape and pushing the building work through endless committees. Plus, obviously he's one of the trustees. But I haven't told them anything about the virtual Santa. I wanted to make sure it could work first.'

'If you hadn't met me, what would you have done about it?' he asked, suddenly curious.

'Found a programmer. Talked to his clients. Offered him a large bonus to get the job done in my timescale.' She shrugged. 'Standard stuff. But it's irrelevant now, because I've met you.'

'How do you know I could…?' he began, and then stopped. 'You talked to some of my clients, didn't you?'

'I couldn't possibly answer that,' she said, making her face impassive and clearing away their empty plates.

He sighed.

'OK. I won't say who I spoke to, but they said that if you run a project then it'll work the way it's supposed to work. No compromises and no mistakes.'

He prided himself on that. 'Yes.'

'And that you call a spade a spade rather

than a digging implement,' she added with a grin.

'What would you call a spade?' he asked.

'That rather depends on the context.'

He smiled. 'A very lawyerly response.'

'It's who I am,' she said.

'No. You're more than your job,' he said. 'You could've just got the rest of your dad's band to come and play some of his most famous songs at the opening. That would've been enough to wow everyone. But you went the extra mile. You're arranging a very special Santa for the kids. It's personal—and I don't mean just for them, I mean for you.'

'That hospital saved my life when I was a baby. I owe them,' she said. 'The virus meant that I was more prone to chest infections when I was really small, and I can remember spending my fourth birthday in hospital with pneumonia, being too ill for a birthday party and balloons and cake. The staff were really kind, but I knew what I was missing. And being in hospital at Christmas is especially hard on kids. They miss out on Santa and all the parties. It's hard on their families, too. I just want to put a bit of sparkle into their day and make a difficult Christmas that little bit better for them.'

'Christmas isn't always good outside hospital,' he said, and then he could have kicked himself for letting the words slip out.

Carissa, just as he'd half expected, homed straight in to the crux of the matter. Even though she'd just brought the box of *macarons* over to the table and looked thrilled when she opened it, she didn't let the pudding distract her. 'Is that why you don't like Christmas?'

No way was he going to discuss that subject with her. 'I don't like the greed and commercialism surrounding Christmas,' he said. Which was true. Just not the whole truth.

'So you don't believe that the spirit of Christmas exists any more?' she asked, putting the *macarons* on a plate.

'Do you?' he asked, throwing the question back at her because he didn't want to admit that the spirit of Christmas had never really existed for him.

'Yes, I do. My parents always made a big deal about Christmas, and I love this time of year. OK, the year they died was different— it's pretty hard to enjoy Christmas when you're fifteen years old and planning a funeral for the two people you love most in the world.' She wrinkled her nose. 'But, other than that year, I've always tried to keep it the way they kept it, full of love and happiness. Just how it should be.'

The complete opposite of the Christmases he remembered. Full of misery and wishing the day was over. Knowing that he wasn't really wanted and was in the way—he'd always had presents, yes, but they'd been on a much smaller scale than those of his cousins because he didn't really belong. He'd been a charity case. Sometimes, as a child, he'd thought he would've been better off in a children's home.

A man who hated Christmas.

It was so far removed from Carissa's own view that it intrigued her. Why didn't Quinn like Christmas? Had he had a tough childhood, maybe? Grown up in a family where Christmas had been a source of tension and worry?

It would explain why he didn't like the commercialism. When money was tight, tempers tended to fray as well. She'd seen the results of that first-hand when she'd helped at the refuge. And yet the women there still tried to make Christmas good for their kids and put their own feelings aside.

She knew she really ought to let this go. Quinn had already shown himself to be a private man. This was none of her business. And she knew, too, that her best friend would call her on it. Erica would say that Carissa had gone straight into Ms Fixit mode as a way of avoiding the fact that she was attracted to Quinn, and it scared her stupid. Fixing things—like making Christmas good again for Quinn—meant that Carissa didn't have to face up to her past.

It was probably true.

Definitely true, she thought wryly. And another way of making Quinn safe to be around.

Yet at the same time it was an irresistible challenge: to show Quinn that there was more to Christmas than just blatant commercialism and greed. And maybe if she could heal whatever hurt was in his heart, it would teach her how to heal the ache in her own heart, too.

'What if I can prove to you that the Christmas spirit is real—that there really is magic out there?' she asked.

'The magic of Christmas?' he scoffed. He didn't believe in it.

But what she was suggesting…it meant spending time together. Getting to know each other. Part of him knew that this was just an excuse for him to spend time with her—something he ought to resist, because he was definitely attracted to her, and with his track record he knew it would end in tears. But then again, if he got to know her better, it would help their business arrangement—he might even be able to improve the Santa project. He looked her straight in the eye. 'What if you can't?'

She lifted her chin. 'Then I'll pay you double for the virtual Santa system.'

'A wager?' He raised an eyebrow. 'OK. Let's make it double or quits. If you can prove it, then I'll build your system free and help you sort out things on the day.'

'Double or quits,' she agreed, and held out her hand.

It was the second time they'd shaken hands on a deal. And this time the tingle in his skin was stronger. Scarily so.

But it was just adrenalin, he told himself. The excitement of the challenge. Nothing to do with her at all...

CHAPTER THREE

This evening. 7 p.m. Meet me at my place.

QUINN READ THE text and frowned. They'd already agreed on a time next week for the training session on his collaborative software. Why did Carissa want to meet him tonight?

Why? he texted back.

Magic of Christmas, proof #1, was the response.

Which told him virtually nothing.

What did Carissa think would prove the magic of Christmas to him?

As far as he was concerned, it simply didn't exist. Christmas was the time when families were forced to spend time together, not really wanting to be there but feeling that they had to do it because it was Christmas and it was expected of them. Resentment, tension and bitterness. Add too much sugary food and a liberal dash of alcohol, and it was no wonder that the emergency departments of most hospitals were full of people who'd ended up coming to blows over the holiday season.

Through his experience with Tabitha, Quinn had learned the hard way to check the dress code before going anywhere so he didn't feel out of place. Would Carissa's idea of Christmas magic involve some kind of ball, maybe?

Do I wear black tie? he texted.

No. Wear something warm because there's meant to be a frost tonight.

So he still knew next to nothing. Great.

It wasn't even as if Carissa was a proper client—one he needed to be nice to for the sake of making a project run smoothly. He knew full well he wasn't going to charge her for his time in setting up the virtual Santa or training her team of volunteers. Not when she was doing something so kind. Charity…but not the cold, grudging kind of charity he'd experienced growing up.

She'd actually thought about this and was trying to do something practical to help. Something that would put a bit of happiness into a difficult day. And it wasn't as if he was going to be spending hours developing something new for her, because he'd already worked on bits of similar systems in the past. It wouldn't take much time at all. Charging her for the work he was doing would feel wrong.

Wear something warm. Frost. Obviously they were going to be doing something outside, he thought. But he had absolutely no idea what.

It turned out to be something Quinn really loathed.

'We're seeing the Christmas lights being switched on?' he guessed, as they got off the tube at Oxford Street and joined the crowd of people thronging up the stairs. 'Oh, now you're kidding me.'

'Bah, humbug.' She nudged him. 'This is great. London by night, all lit up and magical. It's Christmassy. Enjoy it.'

'More like crowds of people pushing each other on the pavements, cars blasting their horns at people to make them get out of the way, and a D-list celeb waiting for people to applaud as they do the terribly difficult job of pressing a switch,' he countered. 'And then all the shops waiting for people to cram into them and queue up for stuff they don't really want but feel forced to buy because it's Christmas and people are expecting presents. Ker-ching.'

She ignored his comments. 'Look at the

trees. All those lights shaped like snowflakes. It's like a real winter wonderland. It's beautiful, Quinn.'

She'd really bought into all the hype, hadn't she? He rolled his eyes. 'Think of all that electricity being wasted. Scarce resources you can't replace.'

She scoffed. 'Don't try to pull the environmentalist card. There's nothing green about someone who lives on takeaway food that comes in cartons you can't even recycle.'

'I guess,' he said.

'I admit you have a point about the crowds. That bit's not much fun. But the lights themselves—surely you can't hate them?' she asked.

'What's the big deal about lights?' he asked.

'They change the atmosphere.'

He didn't see it. At all. Lights were just lights, weren't they? A source of illumination. Nothing special. Nothing magical.

Everyone around him oohed and ahhed as the Christmas lights stretching above the streets were switched on—including Carissa—but it did nothing to change Quinn's mind about the misery of Christmas. A bit of sparkle and glitter was just surface dressing. And it didn't make up for all the tension and short tempers.

As if she'd guessed how fed up he was, she said, 'Let's get away from the crowds.'

They went from Oxford Street down through Regent Street. There were cascades of fairy lights on the outsides of the shops—some gold, some lilac, some silver, some brilliant white—and Carissa clearly loved every bit of the displays. Quinn just wasn't convinced. All he saw was wasted energy and a way of attracting people to spend as much of their disposable income as possible.

Carnaby Street had kooky inflatable decorations, and its famous arches were covered in fairy lights. Piccadilly Circus was as brightly lit as it always was, and the trees in Leicester Square were filled with starbursts that had Carissa cooing in pleasure. And everywhere was heaving with people.

Why on earth was he here? Quinn asked himself. He could be at home, playing a decent arcade game on his console in comfort, drinking coffee and eating pizza straight from the box. Or doing what he really loved, developing a new gadget from concept to prototype. Playing with ideas. Instead, he was trudging through the crowded streets of London with a woman he barely knew, all because she'd set him a wager. A wager that really wasn't a wager, because he had no intention of claiming his winnings in any case. So why didn't he just call this whole thing off?

But then they reached Covent Garden and he saw the delight in Carissa's face.

And he knew exactly why he was here.

Even though wild horses wouldn't make him admit it out loud.

There were fairy lights everywhere, a massive Christmas tree, and a topiary reindeer that was covered in tiny lights. Carissa's expression was as dreamy and glowing as a small child's seeing the magical lights for the very first time.

Quinn was here because of the magic.

Because of *her*.

His head really needed examining, he thought wryly. He didn't need to get involved with anyone. He didn't want to get involved with anyone. And yet here he was, doing something he wouldn't have chosen to do and wasn't enjoying—solely because she'd asked him to be here.

'It's beautiful,' she said softly. 'Look at this, Quinn. Fairy lights everywhere, the street performers and the market stalls and the street musicians. I love this place. But I love it even more at this time of year. It's really magical. Like a real Christmas grotto, life-sized.'

For a second, Quinn almost—*almost*—felt the magic.

But then, as they wandered through the place together, he heard a string quartet playing. Not traditional Christmas carols—oh, no. Instead, they were playing Christmas pop songs. And one Christmas pop song in particular. He nudged Carissa. 'Do you hear that?'

'"Santa, Bring My Baby Home to Me,"' she sang softly.

She'd definitely lied to him about not having any musical ability. Her voice was gorgeous. And now he knew what the song was really about, he could hear the emotion in the words and it actually put a lump in his throat.

'Whenever I hear that song, it always makes me feel close to Mum and Dad,' she said, sounding misty-eyed.

He bit back the caustic comment he'd intended to make—OK, so it would've got his common sense back into place, but at the same time it would've burst her bubble, and he couldn't do that to her. He only just managed to stop himself from pulling her into his arms and giving her a hug. For pity's sake. That wasn't what this was supposed to be about. This was a wager, not a date. He needed to remember that.

Several of the stalls inside the covered areas

were selling Christmas-tree decorations. Carissa browsed through them and bought a snowflake made from tiny white and silver tiles. 'I buy a new decoration for the tree every year,' she said. 'I guess it's a family tradition.'

Another reason why Quinn didn't want to get involved with her. Family traditions really weren't his thing. Apart from the awful Christmases spent growing up, there had been the Christmas he'd spent with Tabitha and her family. A Christmas where they'd had all sorts of 'family traditions' and he'd felt even more out of place than he had with his aunt and uncle. He'd tried his best to fit in, but most of the time it had felt as if they'd been speaking a different language.

He'd thought that he'd managed to bluff his way through it, but once he'd overheard Tabitha's older sister talking to her.

'Don't you think you ought to put the poor thing out of his misery, Tabs?'

How he'd hated that tone of pity. Condescension. How could she call him a 'poor thing'?

'Your bit of rough,' Penelope continued. 'You brought him home to make the parents squirm a bit and worry that you might actually be serious about him—well, he's sweet, and he follows you round with those big puppy-dog eyes, but he's not one of *us*, and you know you'd never stick it out.'

'Don't be ridiculous, Pen.'

He'd walked away at that point, not wanting to hear any more. OK, he might not be enough for Tabitha's family, but he had been sure Tabitha had loved him. She'd just stuck up for him, hadn't she?

How wrong he'd been. He should've stayed a bit longer and heard the rest of the conversation. And then he could've ended it before he'd totally lost his heart.

'Quinn?' Carissa said.

He shook himself. The last thing he wanted was for her to guess at his thoughts. 'Sorry. I glazed over for a minute.'

'I noticed,' she said drily.

'Sorry.' Just to be on the safe side, he changed the subject. 'There's a stall over there selling Christmas paninis. Let's go and get something.'

'My shout,' she said, 'seeing as I dragged you out here.'

'I think I can just about afford to buy you a panini,' he said. And again he was cross with himself. Why was he being on the defensive with her? This was just a hot sandwich. Definitely not a big deal.

Maybe Carissa had picked up his awkward

mood, because she just smiled at him. 'In that case, thank you very much. Cranberry, Brie and bacon for me, please.'

He bought himself a more traditional turkey and stuffing sandwich, and used it as an excuse not to talk. They wandered round the bustle of Covent Garden for a bit longer, then headed back to Leicester Square and caught the tube back to Hyde Park.

'So. Proof number one. Verdict?' she asked on their way back to Grove End Mews.

'I'm not convinced,' he said, ignoring that unsettling moment in the middle of Covent Garden. 'It's not the magic of Christmas—it's more like the misery of Christmas. Money, money, money.'

'Don't think I'm giving up,' she warned. 'I'm going to teach you to believe in the magic of Christmas if it's the last thing I do.'

'Princess Carissa, used to getting her own way?' He knew it was nasty even as the words came out of his mouth, and winced. He was never like this with anyone else. He was known for not saying a lot and just getting on with his job. Why was he so mean and rude to Carissa Wylde? 'Sorry,' he muttered.

'No, you're not. You're in denial. Secretly,' she said, 'I think you really like Christmas, but you just can't admit it because you don't want anyone to know that you might have a soft centre.'

'I don't have a soft centre.' And he definitely didn't like Christmas. Not that he was going to tell her the real reason why. He didn't want her to pity him. Poor little unwanted boy. That wasn't who he was any more, and he refused to let the past define him.

'We'll see,' she said.

She didn't invite him in for a coffee when they reached Grove End Mews, which meant Quinn could escape and restore his equilibrium without her being any the wiser that he'd been so unsettled. 'I'll see you at the training session,' he said.

'OK. And thanks for sorting it all out for me,' she said.

'It's my job,' he said, more to remind himself that this was business and she was off limits.

The training session with Carissa's team went really well. They were nice group of people, clearly all committed to helping out and willing to put the effort in to learn how to use the software. They also clearly all adored Carissa.

Quinn could see why. It would be very easy to let himself adore Carissa. She was sweet, she was bright, and she made the place feel as if it was lit up by a million of the fairy lights she loved so much. He had a nasty feeling that she might be the one woman who could tempt him into giving up his rule of no relationships lasting longer than a fortnight or three dates in a row.

Except then one of the team let something slip. She clammed up again as soon as she realised what she'd said, but it was too late. Quinn had heard. He pretended that he hadn't, to smooth things over—but he'd heard very clearly, and it made him wonder. What exactly was Carissa hiding?

Now wasn't the time to ask questions. But he could wait. He was good at being patient. It went with his job.

He waited until just after breakfast the next morning to text Carissa. *What's Project Sparkle?*

I have no idea what you're talking about, was the slightly haughty reply.

He knew she was lying. OK. If she wouldn't tell him by text, he'd ask her face to face. In a way where she couldn't wriggle out of it. Clearly it was something deeply important to her. But why was she keeping it so far under wraps? What was there to hide?

That evening, he rang her doorbell. His secret weapon was in his hands: a box wrapped in sparkly paper. He'd chosen the paper deliberately. He handed it to her without a word.

'What's this?' she asked.

'Present,' he said economically.

'For me?'

He made a show of looking around the mews. 'I can't see anyone else here it might be for—can you?'

'Funny guy,' she said, rolling her eyes. 'Thank you. Would you like to come up for a cup of tea?'

'Are there brownies?'

She shook her head.

'Any other kind of baked goods?' he asked hopefully.

'Nope.'

Well, it had been worth a try. 'Then in that case a cup of tea would be very nice,' he said.

She made a pot of tea—and, being Carissa, she had a silver tray to go with the teapot, tea strainer and milk jug—then ushered him into her living room. Just as he'd half suspected, the walls were lined with shelves of leather-bound books. Definitely more than the hundred or so that the average British household was meant to contain, according to a news story he'd seen recently; and he'd also bet that she'd read most of them, too.

'I'm surprised you don't have a tree up yet,'

he remarked, as he sat on the pristine leather chesterfield next to her.

'No, I do that on the first day of December.'

Another of her traditions, he guessed. And he was pretty sure that she'd have a proper tree, not an artificial one.

'Am I allowed to open my present now?' she asked, sitting down next to him and indicating the box, which she'd brought in on the tray.

'That was the idea.'

She untied the ribbon and carefully unwrapped the paper. Once she'd revealed the box, she opened it and took off the layer of sparkly tissue paper to reveal fairy lights in the shape of crystal snowflakes. 'Oh! How lovely. Thank you.' She beamed at him. 'Are these for my tree?'

Not unless she planned to have a pocket-sized tree, and someone who loved Christmas as much as Carissa Wylde would no doubt have something much larger. 'No. You plug it into the USB port on your laptop.'

'So these are fairy lights for my laptop?' she asked, sounding surprised.

Had he got this wrong? He shrugged. 'I thought it was very you.'

She smiled at him. 'It is, and it's so sweet of you to think of me and do something so nice.' On impulse, she leaned forward and kissed his cheek. Then she pulled back and looked at him, her blue eyes huge.

He knew that if he rested his hands on her waist and leaned forward, she'd let him kiss her.

Should he?

Would he?

It was so very tempting...

But he wanted some answers first.

'What's Project Sparkle?' he asked softly.

'I don't have the slightest idea what you're talking about.'

She wasn't making eye contact with him any more, and she was touching her nose as he spoke, so he knew she wasn't telling him the truth. But why was she keeping this Project Sparkle stuff such a big secret?

'Carissa...'

'Look, I have no idea where you got this thing about Project Sparkle.'

And Quinn wasn't going to drop her friend in it by telling her.

'I know you do a lot of top-secret stuff,' she continued, 'but it doesn't mean that everyone else in the world is into subterfuge the whole time, you know.'

'True,' he said. 'Did I ever tell you I worked on some lie-detection software?'

And now she looked really panicky. 'I expect that was very useful for your client.'

'It was.' OK. He'd let her off the hook. For now. But he'd keep asking—because Quinn didn't like mysteries. He liked solving puzzles, not ignoring them. And Carissa Wylde had just turned into a very big puzzle. She intrigued him, in lots of ways. And he wanted to find out the truth.

CHAPTER FOUR

QUINN STILL HADN'T worked it out by the time he received Carissa's text.

Busy tonight?

In meetings until seven, he texted back, guessing that this was going to be another of her Christmas things. He didn't want her thinking that he was happy to drop everything for her whenever she pleased.

Tomorrow? she asked.

He was halfway through typing a reply when another text message pinged in.

For MOC proof #2.

Just what he'd half expected. He deleted his half-typed reply and texted instead, OK. Where do I meet you, and what time?

The entrance to Charing Cross station, 7 p.m.

That was fine by him. Dress code?

Warm. And definitely gloves.

Quinn opted for one of his less scruffy pairs of jeans, a black cashmere sweater, black suede boots and a long black coat.

'Perfect,' Carissa said when she met him at the station.

And for once she wasn't wearing a suit and killer heels, he noticed. She was wearing jeans—soft, faded jeans that really highlighted her curves—flat boots and a warm coat. And no briefcase, so either she'd finished work early or she'd had a day off today.

'So where are we going?' he asked as they headed down the Strand.

'Somewhere even a descendant of Ebenezer Scrooge like you will enjoy,' she said.

He laughed. 'Carissa Wylde, are you calling me mean?'

'You're not mean with money,' she said. 'And you're not mean-spirited *exactly*.'

Which made him feel guilty. 'I haven't always been that nice to you,' he admitted.

'Because I pushed you.' She shrugged. 'My

fault. Push someone too hard and eventually they'll push back.'

'So what did you mean?'

'That you don't believe in Christmas. Maybe,' she said thoughtfully, 'you need to be visited by the ghosts of Christmas past, present and future.'

'Are you offering to play the ghost?' he asked. 'Because I can just see you in a floaty white nightdress…'

Then he froze. Why the hell had he said something so stupid? The last thing he wanted was for Carissa to guess that he was attracted to her. He had no intention of acting on that attraction—a woman like Carissa would want more than he was prepared to give, and no way was he laying open his heart and risking it being trampled on. Been there, done that, and knew better now, thank you very much.

But she'd also frozen, and there was colour staining her cheeks. As if she was thinking about it, too—about a huge four-poster bed, and walking across the bedroom to him wearing a demurely cut white nightdress that was anything but demure because the material was sheer enough to let him see the curves of her body in all their glory…

Oh, help. He needed to get his mind off this track. Right now.

'It's far too cold for floaty nightdresses,' she said, shivering theatrically. 'Give me fleecy PJs covered in smiling red-nosed reindeer any day.'

He was glad that she'd defused the situation. Though his tongue still felt as if it were stuck to the roof of his mouth. He really hoped she didn't expect him to have a conversation with her, because right now he simply wasn't capable of it.

She stopped outside a beautiful eighteenth-century building, all cream stone and columns and balustrades and tall windows. 'I give you proof of the magic of Christmas, mark two,' she said. 'The skating rink at Somerset House.'

The square courtyard outside the house had been turned into a huge ice rink. There was a massive Christmas tree at the front of the house, covered in lights and baubles. Music was playing—Christmas music, Quinn noted wryly, meaning that Carissa's father's song was bound to make at least one appearance later—and there were huge white snowflakes projected onto the surface of the ice, their surroundings lit up in different colours.

'I forgot to ask,' Carissa said. 'Do you skate?'

'I can ski,' he said. 'It can't be too different.'

'Probably not. It's just a question of balance.'

'Don't tell me you did dancing on ice skates as a child,' he said.

'No. But my parents used to take me skating every Christmas when I was small,' she said. 'And, yes, I did have ballet lessons.'

Picturing her wearing a tutu was really not a good idea. Especially given that he was a novice skater; he really didn't need an extra distraction to help him fall flat on his face.

'"Lay on, Macduff,"' he said.

She laughed. 'Don't be so melodramatic. It's not a duel to the death. It's Christmas ice-skating. It's *fun*.'

She took his hand and drew him over to the entrance. And he was glad that they were both wearing gloves. He had a feeling that the touch of her skin against his would do serious damage to his peace of mind.

Being Carissa—organised to military precision—she'd already bought their tickets and their time slot was just coming up.

'Let me know how much I owe you for my ticket,' he said as he put his skates on.

'Buy me a hot chocolate and a cinnamon pretzel, and we'll call it quits,' she said.

'As you wish.'

She tipped her head on one side and regarded him narrowly. 'Were you just quoting a movie at me, Quinn?'

'Movie? What movie?' He didn't have a clue what she was on about.

'Hmm. Never mind,' she said, and skated in circles round him.

Quinn was much less sure of himself. He felt like a wobbly newborn deer, with his legs not quite under control on the ice. He wasn't sure he could go in a straight line, let alone follow her in those circles. Particularly when she changed direction and skated backwards. 'You're showing off,' he accused.

'Showing off? *Moi*?' She laughed, and executed a perfect pirouette, her arms up like a ballerina's.

People around them actually clapped, and Quinn wanted the ice to open up and let him sink through it. He was just about to make a total fool of himself.

But then she took his hand. 'Sorry. That was a bit mean. I didn't intend to make you feel stupid. I just love ice-skating. It's such fun.'

Again, he saw that childlike joy he'd glimpsed on her face when she'd seen the Christmas lights at Covent Garden. And he envied her that ability to see the wonder in things. He'd never felt that joy as a child; he'd always been too conscious of who he was. The boy who'd been dumped on his aunt and uncle because his mother had been off chasing her dreams and nobody had a clue who his father was. He'd always been so conscious of the need to be visibly grateful for their charity—and to work hard so that he could escape from it—that he hadn't had time to stop and see things.

He shook himself. Enough of the pity party. The past was the past and he couldn't change it. But what he could do was make sure that he didn't put himself in a position where he felt at a disadvantage.

So why had he agreed to go ice-skating, as a novice, with someone who clearly excelled at it? *Idiot*, he castigated himself.

'Stop frowning, Quinn,' she said softly. 'We're meant to be having fun.'

Fun.

Yeah.

Right.

She took his hand. 'If you can ski, that means you have good balance and your core's strong. So come on. You can do this. Just put one foot in front of the other and glide.'

Glide. 'Uh-huh.' He tried a couple of staccato strokes and simply succeeded in sending up a spray of ice shards.

'Let yourself go,' she said softly.

That was definitely something he couldn't do. He'd had too many years of total self-discipline. From not letting himself cry in his childhood, through to not letting anyone stomp on his heart as an adult, after Tabitha.

Doggedly, he continued the staccato strokes and made a total hash of gliding over the ice.

'Lean on me,' she said, and slipped her arm round his waist.

Oh, help.

Now he was really aware of Carissa's scent. Something floral, overlaid with vanilla and underlaid with something that smelled like fresh linen.

Somehow, his arm ended up round her shoulders.

And somehow he wasn't making those staccato little strokes any more. With her by his side, holding him close, he was gliding. Almost like floating on air. And it felt amazing. He wasn't sure if he felt more like Peter Pan, or like Jack in *Titanic* while he stood on the bow of the ship with Rose, encouraging her to feel that she was flying—a scene he'd sneered at when he'd been forced to watch the movie with a girlfriend, but now he was seeing it in a completely different light. The only time he'd felt like this before had been when he'd learned to ski and he'd braved the ski jump for the first time—the incredible feeling of weightlessness and the rush of the air round him.

Something clicked. The gliding motion of the skates, the sparkle of the lights, the scent of hot chocolate and pretzels, the sound of sleigh-bells in a jolly Christmas song, the warmth of Carissa's arm round his waist... This was perfect.

And Quinn was shocked to realise just how much he was enjoying himself.

Carissa had clearly guessed, because she asked softly, 'So do you admit that it's magical?'

'Yes, this is fabulous—but it has absolutely nothing to do with Christmas.'

She coughed. 'That's a massive Christmas tree in front of the rink, unless I'm very much mistaken and it's really an inflatable penguin.'

Quinn just about suppressed a grin. He liked her style of sarcasm. 'But it doesn't have to be Christmas for there to be an ice rink,' he countered.

'Stop being so stubborn and just admit it,' she said, drawing him to a halt and spinning round in front of him so she could look into his face.

Carissa's blue eyes were huge. Her mouth was perfect. And Quinn really, really wanted to kiss her. So much that he couldn't stop himself dipping his head to brush his mouth against hers.

And it felt as if he'd just died and gone to heaven. Part of him groaned at the cliché, but most of him knew the truth of it. He'd wanted to kiss Carissa Wylde almost since the first day he'd met her.

'OK. I admit it,' he said softly. 'This is magical.' And he didn't just mean the skating rink. He meant kissing her.

It was the first time a man had kissed her in three years.

It should have sent Carissa running straight for cover.

Yet there had been nothing demanding and angry about Quinn's mouth. His kiss had been gentle and sweet—asking rather than demanding, and soft rather than punishing.

And right now he looked as shocked as she felt.

Swept off her feet.

This is magical. The words echoed through her head. The way his mouth had made her lips tingle. The Christmas-tree lights and the scent of hot chocolate. The Christmassy music playing.

Yes, this was magical.

Unable to help herself, she reached up to lay the flat of her palm against his cheek.

Her glove was butter-soft leather, incredibly thin and pliant—and it was very much an unwanted barrier between his skin and hers. She wanted to touch him. Needed to touch him. Needed him to kiss her again.

'Quinn,' she whispered, and he dipped his head again. Brushed his mouth against hers all over again. And she was shaking so much that she had to hold on to him to stop herself falling over on the ice. She felt as if she were spinning in an endless pirouette, faster and faster and totally out of control.

This had to stop.

And yet she didn't want it to stop. She wanted him to keep kissing her like this, with his arms wrapped round her—cradling her, cherishing her, keeping her warm and close.

Another skater bumped into them, but somehow Quinn managed to keep them both upright. And, even though Carissa was the more experienced skater of the two of them, it was Quinn who got her back to the edge of the rink, to the area where they could take their skates off.

He didn't look at her as he removed his skates and changed back into his shoes. And

Carissa knew that it was going to be hideously awkward between them now.

What an idiot she'd been.

Why hadn't she just pulled away? Why had she even made this ridiculous bet with him in the first place? Why couldn't she just have commissioned him to work on the virtual Santa project and left it at that?

She realised that he was looking at her, as if he'd been speaking and was waiting for her to reply.

'Sorry, I was miles away—I missed what you said,' she admitted, avoiding his gaze.

'I said I believe I owe you a hot chocolate and a cinnamon pretzel.'

Ah. So that was the way he was going to play it. Pretend that the moment on the ice had never happened. OK. That worked for her. Because the alternative right now was way too scary to contemplate.

She put on her brightest smile. 'That would be lovely. Thank you so much.'

He didn't say much while they queued for their drink and their food. He waited until they were walking along the Embankment, watching the reflected lights sparkle on the surface of the Thames, before saying, 'Now tell me about Project Sparkle.'

She almost dropped her hot chocolate. He was still thinking about that?

'I know it exists, and I know you're behind it,' he said. 'So it's a bit pointless to keep trying to deny it.'

She couldn't argue with that. And he clearly wasn't going to give up until she told him. 'Can I ask you to keep this as confidential as you keep your other work?'

'Yes.'

'Yes, I can ask you, or, yes, you'll keep it confidential?' Being a lawyer, she was aware of the ambiguity. She couldn't afford any ambiguity right now. Not over this.

'Both,' he said.

'OK.' She blew out a breath. 'Project Sparkle… It's about making a difference.'

'So you're not actually a lawyer, then?'

'I'm a qualified solicitor and I work in a practice specialising in contract law,' she corrected. 'But I job-share my role with a colleague who has two young children. It suits us both. She gets to spend time with her kids, and I get time to run Project Sparkle.'

'That's what's behind the virtual Santa?'

She nodded. 'But not the building of the new ward. That's all Dad. He started the ball rolling on it years ago, and after he was killed the trustees agreed to make sure his plans were completed.'

'So Project Sparkle is the extra stuff—the bits on top?' he asked.

'Yes and no. My parents left me a lot of money,' she said. 'More than I can use. And I never wanted to be a celebrity child, followed around by the media just because my dad was a rock star. I don't want to spend my life like a WAG, going to parties and having my nails done and sitting in a tanning booth and exchanging gossip. I want to make the world a better place. Be a…' She paused. 'Don't you dare laugh at this,' she warned.

He looked perfectly serious. 'I won't.'

'I want to be a fairy godmother, except what I do is real. I want to put a bit of fairy dust into people's lives. *Sparkle*.'

'And make yourself feel good in the process.'

She frowned, shocked that he could think that of her. 'No. It's not about me. It's about making a difference. Actually, everyone involved with Project Sparkle signed a confidentiality agreement—so I need to know who told you, to make sure they remember that in future.'

'I'd rather not reveal my source,' he said. 'The person who let it slip didn't mean any harm. They assumed I already knew, given that I was working on the virtual Santa. And when they realised I didn't know about it at all and what they'd just done... I could see them panicking. So I pretended I hadn't heard a thing.'

'That's nice of you,' she said, 'but it still leaves me with a potential leak. I guess I need to do a general reminder to everyone, then.'

'Why do they have to sign a confidentiality agreement? Surely if you tell the press and get coverage for your projects, other people might come and donate money or time or what have you, to make the most of the project?' he asked.

'Or maybe the press will dig around for a story that sells more copies for them,' she said. 'I've been very lucky and I've had a very privileged life—but a lot of people haven't been that lucky, and do you really think they want their personal business splashed all over the press and people making judgements?' She shook her head. 'My way means they get to keep their dignity. It isn't charity and rubbing their noses in it. It's giving them a hand up rather than a handout. Making a quiet difference to people's lives. I'm not expecting any thanks or any publicity. Being able to make a difference is reward enough.'

'So you're being a do-gooder.' His face shuttered. 'The rich girl giving to the underprivileged.'

'That's insulting,' she said. She hadn't wanted him to laugh at her—but she hadn't expected him to be so hostile about it. 'What's so wrong with wanting to do something nice for people?'

If he explained—because his aunt and uncle had been 'nice' to him, taking him in when his mother had dumped him on their doorstep, but always making him feel like a charity case—then Carissa would start to pity him.

No way would he let that happen. He didn't want pity from her. Ever.

He flicked a dismissive hand. 'Whatever.'

But then she did something that shocked him.

She flinched.

He frowned. 'Carissa? What's wrong?'

'Nothing.'

But he could hear the tremble in her voice. And he could see a flicker of fear in her face as she turned away. And her shoulders were slightly hunched as she walked away.

What had just happened?

OK, he'd been sniping at her because his past had come back to get in his way yet again—but why had she flinched like that? He hadn't done anything. Just flapped his hand. There was something more to it this than met the eye. A lot more. And he needed to get to the bottom of it. Make things right again.

He hurried after her. 'Carissa? Wait. Please.' He deliberately made his voice as gentle as he could. He wanted to put his hand on her arm, but he had a feeling that she wouldn't take it the way he meant it, as reassurance. And he really didn't want to see her flinch like that again. 'Carissa? I'm sorry. Please. Talk to me.'

She did at least stop and turn to face him, but her expression was filled with wariness. Someone had made her wary. But who? She'd just been talking about her privileged upbringing, and everything she'd ever told him about her parents and her grandparents made him sure that she'd been deeply loved.

So who had hurt her? Why would anyone hurt someone as sweet and kind and giving as Carissa?

'It doesn't matter,' she said, shrugging and looking away.

'It does,' he said. 'Carissa, I apologise. I know I'm in the wrong. But I think there's something else, too—something that isn't me.'

'It doesn't matter,' she said again.

Oh, yes, it did. It mattered hugely. And he needed to make this better. 'Right now,' he said, 'I'd like to hug you. But I think that's going to spook you, and I don't want to do that. So instead I'd like you to talk to me. It's up to you where we talk—if you'd rather, we can be in a public place where there are plenty of people round us and you feel safe—but I need to know what I did to make you look as scared as hell, because I never want to make you look like that again.'

In the end, she agreed to go back to his place. She didn't say a word on the way back to Grove End Mews, but once he'd made her a mug of coffee and rustled up a packet of biscuits, he was careful to sit on a chair rather than next to her on the sofa. Giving her enough space to feel safe.

'Talk to me, Carissa,' he said, as gently as he could.

CHAPTER FIVE

CARISSA KNEW SHE should've made an excuse. She should've said something to put him off the scent.

Except Quinn O'Neill wasn't the kind of man who gave up easily—or at all. He'd pushed her into telling him about Project Sparkle, and now he was pushing her into telling him about the thing she never, but never, talked about.

The thing that made her feel ashamed.

Grubby.

Pathetic.

She didn't even talk about it to the three people who actually knew about it, so telling someone she hardly knew was next to impossible. The words caught in her throat.

But Quinn simply waited for her to speak.

Not the kind of aggressive silence that pushed you into filling it; this was an accepting silence. One that said it was OK to pause and collect her thoughts. That he didn't mind waiting. That it was going to be just fine.

She couldn't look him in the eye—she was too ashamed—and it was much easier just to stare into the mug of coffee she held in her cupped hands. But finally Carissa began to talk.

'It was three years ago. I was twenty-four. I met Justin at a party—a friend of a friend. He was in the City. Charming. Witty. Handsome. A high flyer.'

And with a temper he'd kept hidden from her for months. Or maybe she'd just let herself ignore the signs, not wanting to see them or believe the truth.

Still staring into her coffee cup, she said, 'We'd dated for six months when we moved in together. To his place. It was probably still too soon and I should've been more sensible, but I thought…' She closed her eyes and whispered, 'I thought he loved me. He said he loved me.'

'And you're used to being loved.'

There wasn't an edge to Quinn's voice. No judgement. Just understanding.

She nodded. 'My family's close. My parents were brilliant. My grandparents, my aunts and uncles, my cousins. There's never been any big falling-out in my family. Sure, they disagree about things and sometimes they shout, but normally everyone just talks things through. There's never been any door-slamming or tantrums or not talking to people for months.'

'And Justin was a door-slammer?'

She swallowed. 'Sort of.'

Quinn was fast. He picked up what she wasn't saying. 'You had to tell people that you walked into a door.' Again, there was no judgement in his voice. Just softness. Security.

Which made it easy to answer him. To admit the truth. 'Yes.' Though there was more to it than that. She swallowed hard. 'The first time. He was…' She paused, choosing her words precisely. 'More careful after that.' She grimaced. 'It was my own fault. I knew I should tread on eggshells around him if he'd had a bad day at work.'

'No,' Quinn said. 'You talk when you've had a bad day at work. You push yourself hard at the gym, or your eat your way through a whole tub of ice cream, or you play music too loud, or you play a mindless shoot-'em-up arcade game. Whatever it takes to unload the stress. But you don't hit people. *Ever.*'

But Justin had. After that first time it had been where the bruises wouldn't show.

'Did you call the police?' Quinn asked.

She shook her head wearily. 'What was the point? It would've been his word against mine.'

'Not if you had bruises.'

That was half the problem. 'It wasn't always physical.' And Justin's words had chipped away at her confidence until she'd started to believe that she deserved the way he treated her. That it was her fault. That she provoked him into behaving that way.

'Carissa,' Quinn said softly. 'Please tell me you had someone to talk to.'

'I was so ashamed,' she said. 'I was supposed to have this perfect life—I was close to qualifying as a solicitor, with a dream career ahead of me. I was living in a fabulous flat in a posh part of the city with a rich, successful boyfriend who adored me. I had nothing to worry about in the world.'

Nothing except how to avoid the arguments. How to stop Justin's temper flaring.

'You picked the wrong guy,' Quinn said. 'It happens. And when it happens it's OK to say you got it wrong and walk away.'

'I was going to leave him,' she said. 'And I was going to tell him after I'd done it. Which I know is cowardly.'

'No, it was sensible,' Quinn said, 'because otherwise you would've given him the chance to bully you out of it.'

Which he'd done anyway. Because she'd been stupid. She hadn't taken quite enough care. 'I must've let something slip, because he came home early from work that day and caught me packing.' She dragged in a breath. 'He, um, didn't want me to leave.'

Quinn said nothing.

'The trust fund was going to come through in a couple more months. When I turned twenty-five.'

Quinn still said nothing.

'Justin was in a mess at work—he'd brokered a deal that went wrong. He'd covered it up, but he knew he was going to lose his job if he couldn't pay back the money he'd lost. I was a lawyer, so I should've been able to find a way to break my trust fund and help him out.'

'From what you've said about your family, I don't think they would've agreed. Except,' Quinn said, 'to save you from being hurt any more.'

They hadn't known about it. She'd been too ashamed to tell them. She still hadn't told them. Only her best friend, her friend who shared her job and her PA knew. She'd sworn them to silence. Begged them not to tell anyone.

'He broke my arm,' she said. 'He wouldn't let me go to hospital that night. But I went the next morning on my way to work.'

She heard his hiss of indrawn breath. 'You were in pain with a broken arm *all night*?'

She hadn't had much choice. Saying a single word about it would only have made Justin angry again. 'I took some paracetamol.' Not that it had done much to touch the pain. She'd lain awake all night, wondering how her life had gone so wrong and how on earth she was ever going to escape the nightmare. At the darkest point of the night she'd even considered that taking a few more paracetamol might be the only way out. But then the first grey light of dawn had filtered through the curtains and she'd known that way wasn't for her.

'Right now,' Quinn said softly, 'I really want to beat your ex to a pulp. Except violence doesn't solve anything, so I won't do that.' He paused. 'And I also want to hold you close. Except I don't want to scare you.'

She looked at him then. 'You don't despise me?'

'Of course not.' He frowned. 'Why would I despise you, Carissa?'

Did he really want her to spell it out? 'For being weak.'

He shook his head. 'You were used to being loved. Treasured. When Justin hurt you, you were probably so shocked that you couldn't think straight. So, no, you weren't weak. And, no, I don't despise you.'

She had to gulp in air to stop herself from weeping. Because she couldn't believe that he didn't despise her. Not when she despised herself so much.

'Carissa,' he said softly.

And there was no judgement, no censure in his tone. Just gentleness and acceptance.

She dragged in another shaky breath. 'Then in that case I think, yes, please, I'd like you to hold me.'

Immediately, Quinn took the coffee from her hands with gentle fingers and set the mug on the low table. Then he scooped her up, took her seat and settled her on his lap with his arms wrapped round her—not so loosely that she felt he was just humouring her, and not so tightly that she felt panicky and trapped. Just warm and strong and supportive. He didn't say a single word, just held her.

It would be so easy to let herself cry into his broad shoulder.

But she'd promised herself she'd never cry again. Not over Justin. Not over the past.

He stroked her hair, and the tenderness of the gesture nearly made her crack.

'Please tell me you left him,' Quinn said softly.

'I didn't go back,' she said. 'I left everything at his flat. The nurse… She knew something was wrong. I wouldn't tell her what had happened, but she made me call my best friend from the hospital. Erica came and she made me tell her everything. And she said I was never, ever, ever going to have him anywhere near me again.'

'You took out an injunction against him?'

'I…' She blew out a breath. 'Erica wanted me to. You can get an *ex parte* injunction without the other party being given notice, pending a full hearing. We both knew that. But…' she swallowed '…I was so ashamed. And I didn't want my parents' names dragged through the mud. I didn't want the press getting hold of the injunction and spreading the story, talking about Pete Wylde's daughter being battered. I didn't want people associating that sort of thing with Mum and Dad.'

'But can't you make injunctions private, so the papers can't report it?'

'Not back then you couldn't.' She grimaced. 'Justin could've denied it and pushed it through to trial. And I had no proof.'

'You had a broken arm,' Quinn pointed out.

'Which I could have got from a fall. Justin's articulate. And charming. He could've talked the magistrate round. Because, after all, I'm a pop star's daughter. I'm spoiled, used to getting my own way. High maintenance. What's to say that I didn't threaten to throw myself down the stairs if he didn't do what I wanted—and then, after he called my bluff and I did it and broke my own arm, I claimed he'd pushed me, just to get my own back?'

'You're *not* high maintenance,' Quinn said.

That sounded personal. Carissa looked at him, curious, but his expression was inscrutable—as if he realised that he'd just slipped up and didn't want her to push it further.

Before she could ask, he said, 'If you'd taken him to court, it might have scared him into getting help and stopped him doing the same thing to someone else.'

Erica had said the same thing. 'I know.' The guilt seeped through her even now. 'And I'm ashamed of that, too,' she whispered. 'But I'm trying to make amends.'

His face was full of questions, but she wasn't ready to answer any more. 'Enough, Quinn,' she said. 'I'm tired.'

He cupped her cheek for a fleeting moment. The same way that she'd touched him at the skating rink, just before he'd kissed her. But she knew this was meant to be a gesture of comfort, not enticement.

'If you want to stay tonight,' he said, 'give

me a second to put clean sheets on my bed and I'll sleep on the couch.'

He'd really do that for her?

How good it would be to lean on someone. But she'd made that mistake with Justin. She knew Quinn wasn't like Justin—he had a good heart—but she couldn't let herself make that mistake again. She needed to keep her independence. 'Thank you, but I'm only three doors down,' she said. 'I'll be fine on my own.'

'Can I walk you home?'

'All three doors away?' she asked wryly.

'It'd make me feel better,' he said.

She rested her forehead against his briefly, then climbed off his lap. Right now she needed to stand on her own two feet again—literally as well as metaphorically. To prove to herself that she could do it—that she wasn't the weak, despicable mess she'd been three years ago. 'You're a good man, Quinn O'Neill. You have a good heart.'

'Hmm,' he said, and walked her home.

He waited for her to unlock her front door. 'If you can't sleep tonight,' he said, 'call me. Or come over.'

Tempting. But she wouldn't. She'd already told him way too much. Right now she needed to be on her own. Regroup. Get her walls safely up again. 'Thank you,' she said, meaning it.

* * *

Quinn didn't sleep properly that night. He could still see the fear in Carissa's face. How many times had her ex moved his hand impatiently like that as a prelude to hitting her?

That bright, sparkly exterior was designed to deflect attention away from the fact that she'd lost her ability to trust. And he was pretty sure that Project Sparkle helped her just as much as the people she made life better for—it proved to her that the world could be a good place. Yet, at the same time, it must make her doubt herself.

She had just as much baggage as he did.

Which was another reason why he really ought to stay away from her. She needed someone who could support her, not someone who was flooded with his own doubts. Well, he'd find a way of backing off without damaging her any more, and go back to what he was good at. Being on his own.

But Carissa turned up on his doorstep at half past nine the next morning with lemon drizzle cake. Still warm. Smelling tart and sweet all at the same time. Mouthwatering.

Like her.

He damped the thought down before it got out of control and got him into trouble.

'I ran out of chocolate,' she said. 'I hope this is an acceptable alternative.'

Quinn wondered if she baked every time she felt low. Hadn't he read somewhere that the scent of vanilla was meant to make you feel good?

'Very acceptable,' he said. 'Come in and have a mug of coffee.'

So much for putting distance between them. Yet again his mouth had run away with him.

But something about her drew him to her. Not the vulnerability—he wasn't arrogant enough to think that he was the answer to every woman's prayers—but the warmth, the sweetness, the essential Carissa-ness of her.

Today she wasn't in the suit and killer heels, and the briefcase wasn't in evidence; given that it was after most people would be at their desks in the City, clearly it wasn't one of her office days. He wished it had been—because in her office gear she was far less approachable and it was easier to resist her. Today she was all softness—faded jeans, a cashmere sweater, and her hair was tied loosely in a ponytail by a chiffon ribbon rather than pinned back in the formal French pleat she wore for work. It reminded him of the way she'd looked last night at the ice skating rink.

Two seconds before he'd kissed her.

And he really needed to stop remembering how that had felt.

'Are you sure I'm not interrupting your work?' she asked.

Actually, she was. It was the perfect excuse to get rid of her. So why on earth wasn't he using it? 'It's fine,' he said, and ushered her up to the kitchen.

He made two mugs of coffee and cut two slices of the cake. Which tasted even better than it smelled. He could get addicted to this stuff.

'So what are you doing this morning—if you can tell me?' she asked.

'What I can tell you is that it's to do with surveillance systems.'

'Surveillance systems.' She looked thoughtful. 'Could you make one for a house?'

She wanted a surveillance system? Given what she'd told him last night, the question made him frown. 'What's worrying you, Carissa? Is your ex stalking you? Because, if he is, I know people who can have a quiet word with him and scare the hell out of him to make sure he leaves you alone in future. And, yes, of course I can do a surveillance system for you.'

'He's not stalking me.' She lifted her chin. 'And I'm fine.'

Quinn knew a lie when he heard one. The

second bit was definitely a lie. She wasn't fine at all.

'I wasn't asking you about a system for my house,' she said.

'Whose house, then?'

She bit her lip. 'I need to think about this. Anyway, that's not why I came to see you. I wanted to apologise for yesterday.'

'There's nothing to apologise for,' he said.

'Thank you.'

But there was something else. He could tell from the way she was sitting that there was something on her mind—something making her a little tense. 'Why do I get the feeling that the cake was softening me up for another of your alleged proofs of the magic of Christmas?' he asked

'Not at all,' she said. 'Actually, I'm after your biceps.'

All his blood drained south and he had an immediate vision of lifting her up and carrying her to his bed. Not that it was going to happen. Given what her ex had done, Quinn knew he was lucky that she trusted him to be nearer to her than a ten-foot bargepole would allow.

'Why exactly do you need my biceps?' he asked. Then a really nasty thought hit him. 'You're not doing a calendar or something, are you, to raise funds for Project Sparkle?'

She laughed. 'No, but you'd hold your own in a group of bare-chested firefighters on a calendar photo. My PA thinks that smart-is-the-new-sexy headline was spot on.'

'I wasn't fishing,' Quinn said loftily, but secretly he was flattered. Very flattered. 'So why do you need my biceps?'

'To haul a tree about.'

Oh, no. 'Would this be a Christmas tree?' he asked, knowing that the answer was perfectly obvious, so the question didn't actually need asking in the first place.

'It's the first of December today. I always put my tree up on the first of December.'

'Right. So this means a trip to a forest or something?'

'No—a market in the East End,' she said. 'Though I plan to drive. We're not lugging a tree up and down the escalators and on the Tube.'

Market? He struggled to compute that one. 'But you're not the type to shop at a market.'

'Don't be such a snob,' she said crisply.

'Carissa, you live in a mews house in Belgravia, you're a lawyer, and you wear designer clothes,' he pointed out. 'The only market you'd shop in would be a posh farmers' market.'

She folded her arms. 'I'll have you know

that I come from East End barrow-boy stock—generations of them. My family's had a fruit stall in an East End market for years and years and years.'

He blinked at her. 'But I thought your grandfather was a barrister? Are you trying to tell me your family's not posh?'

'Mum's is,' she said, 'but Dad's isn't.'

And her accent was completely cut glass. No way would she fit in with people who spoke broad Cockney. 'Don't you feel out of place?'

'What, when I visit Nan and Poppy?' She laughed. 'No way—I'm a Wylde. Totally one of them. They all loved my mum and they all get on well with Granny and Gramps, too.'

He couldn't quite process this. The posh girl was actually from a very ordinary family?

She grinned at his obvious confusion. 'Where do you think I learned to bake brownies like that? Poppy had a fruit stall and Nan had a cake stall. I used to help on a Saturday morning when I was little by polishing the red apples for Poppy or helping Nan bake.'

'Poppy?' Wasn't that a girl's name? Her aunt—or her grandmother's partner?

'Nan and Pops,' she explained. 'My paternal grandparents. Except I used to call my grandfather "Poppy" when I was about two and it kind of stuck.'

Cute. Irresistibly cute. Quinn could just imagine Carissa as a toddler.

And that scared him even more. He wasn't interested in kids. Never had been. He'd never wanted them. So why was he suddenly thinking about toddlers and wondering what Carissa's children would look like?

He needed to change the subject. Fast. Before his head got *really* carried away with the fantasy of Carissa and children.

So her dad's family had a market stall. 'Didn't they expect your dad to go into the family business?'

'No. Dad was the youngest of four, and all he ever did was sing. He picked up his teacher's guitar at infant school and taught himself to play. She realised he was a born musician and Nan and Poppy always supported him.' She smiled. 'They told him to follow his dreams—and if he didn't make it, they'd still be there.'

What would it be like to have that kind of family? Close-knit, supportive?

His own family had been dismissive of his endless messing about with computers, convinced there was no future in it—and even pointing out the success of giants such as Bill Gates and Steve Jobs hadn't convinced them that Quinn would have a much better and more lucrative career in software development than in working seven days a week in a corner shop. And they hadn't quite forgiven him for being right. Particularly during the recession. He'd tried to do the right thing and it had gone badly, badly wrong.

And he'd *really* picked the wrong topic of conversation here.

'That's nice,' he said neutrally.

'So can I borrow your biceps?'

'In exchange for cake that I've already eaten?'

She wrinkled her nose, and she looked so cute that he really had to rein himself back. 'That sounds a bit bad. You *can* say no.'

'What, and leave you to lug a tree about on your own?'

'I won't be on my own. Someone'll give me a hand. We look after our own in the East End.'

A Cockney girl with a posh voice. Quinn still couldn't quite get his head around that.

And he also wasn't that keen on the idea of some other guy impressing her with his biceps.

'Let's go and get your tree,' he said.

CHAPTER SIX

CARISSA'S CAR TURNED out to be an estate car in soft gunmetal grey. It was a prestige marque, and bore a discreet personalised number plate; though it surprised Quinn, as he'd expected her to drive a little red sports car with a soft top.

'What, one you can't fit anything in and you can only ever have one passenger? Totally impractical,' Carissa scoffed, when he said as much.

True. But Carissa was wealthy. Wouldn't she have a car like that just for fun and sunny days? 'You don't have a second car?' he asked.

'No. A car's just a means of getting somewhere.' She shrugged. 'I really don't get why men think cars are so special.'

'It's Y-chromosome stuff,' Quinn said, and shut up.

Luckily Carissa was a confident driver, so he could relax in the passenger seat. And she'd clearly driven this route often enough to know exactly where she was going, not needing to use a GPS system. She was also confident in parking, he noticed—though she'd also parked in a restricted area. 'Aren't you supposed to have a permit to park here?' he asked.

'Yes. And I'll have a visitor's permit in a couple of minutes,' she said.

'Visitor's permit?'

'Nan and Poppy live right there.' She pointed to an ordinary terraced house. 'Dad would've bought them somewhere bigger, but they refused to move from the house where he was born, so he gave in and bought it for them.' She smiled. 'And a little cottage by the sea. Which is why in the summer I got to make sandcastles every single day when I was little.'

He was surprised at how normal Carissa's upbringing had been, give that she was a pop star's daughter. And he was also envious. Living in the Midlands, he'd been miles from the sea. And holidays had been pretty much out of the question, given the shop's schedule. He'd been almost ten the first time he'd been to the seaside.

She climbed out of the car. 'Coming?'

And now she was planning to introduce him to her family? Oh, help. He'd been here before and it had been a disaster. 'Won't I be in the way?' he asked, hoping the panic didn't show in his voice.

'How, when you're my hired muscle?' She paused. 'By the way, Nan's brownies are better than mine.'

He was out of the car two seconds later, and she laughed. 'You are *so* easily bought.'

'Yeah, yeah,' he said, rolling his eyes, and followed her down the path.

Carissa was greeted with a hug by an older woman who bore a strong resemblance to her. They were joined by a man waving a piece of paper at her—clearly the parking permit, because she said, 'I'll just put this in the windscreen. I'll be back in a tick.' Though to Quinn's relief she introduced them before she went. 'Nan, Poppy, this is Quinn O'Neill, my neighbour. I'm borrowing his biceps to lug my tree around. Quinn, these are my grandparents, Tom and Mary Wylde.'

'Come in,' Mary said.

Quinn followed her into the kitchen—which smelled as gloriously of baking as Carissa's—and took up her offer of a seat at the table. As Carissa's grandmother put the kettle on, he could feel her grandparents sizing him up.

'So you live in Grove End?' Tom asked.

He nodded. 'I moved in a couple of weeks ago.'

'Work in the City, do you?' Tom asked, his eyes narrowing slightly.

Quinn could guess where this was going. 'No. I work in computers,' he said. Which was true—just not the whole truth.

Tom Wylde looked visibly relieved at the fact he wasn't a City high flyer.

Although Quinn was pretty sure that Carissa hadn't told her family exactly what had happened with Justin, he also guessed that the Wyldes had been suspicious of the man. And with good reason.

'I'm not dating Carissa,' he said, to reassure them. Also true, though it was skating a bit on the borders of the truth. The couple of times he and Carissa had gone out together had been purely to do with their wager; and yet they'd ended up kissing at the skating rink. 'But I am working with her on a project,' he added.

He'd used the word deliberately, and he saw the Wyldes relax even more. 'What kind of project?' Mary asked, clearly trying to sound casual.

'I believe she has a confidentiality clause,' he said, 'so I'll just say "fairy dust" and leave it at that, if I may.'

They nodded approvingly at him.

Carissa strolled into the kitchen at that point. 'Nan, Poppy, I hope you're not giving

Quinn a hard time. He's being very kind and helping me.'

'Not *that* kind. She's paying me in brownies,' Quinn said.

Carissa rolled her eyes. 'I knew you'd bring that up. Nan, I told him you make better brownies than I do.'

'Hmm.' But Mary Wylde took a tin from a cupboard, put brownies on a plate, and offered them to Quinn along with the strongest cup of tea he'd ever had in his life.

She waited for his verdict.

'Am I allowed to say it's a tie?' Quinn asked, when he'd eaten the first one.

'No,' Carissa said, not letting him off the hook.

'That isn't very fair. If I say your grandmother's are better, then I'm insulting you. If I say yours are better, then I'm insulting your grandmother,' Quinn pointed out. 'Either way, I lose.'

There was amusement in Tom's face.

Carissa folded her arms, leaned against the worktop and stared at him.

And she looked right at home here, Quinn thought. Where she belonged.

He suppressed his envy. He'd never really felt that he belonged anywhere. Yet Carissa was clearly as relaxed and comfortable in a modest terraced house as she was in a posh mews house in Belgravia. She could fit in anywhere, whereas he was just a fake. 'Right. Yours are squidgier in the middle, Carissa, and yours are crisper on the outside, Mrs Wylde. They're different, but equal.'

'Good answer, son,' Tom said, and patted him on the shoulder. 'Have you had a word with Big Jake about your tree, Carissa?'

'Last week,' she confirmed. 'He's got me a seven-footer.'

'He'll see you right,' Tom said with a smile. He looked at Quinn. 'Big Jake's dad started the stall not long after I took over ours. They're three down from us—bedding plants in the summer, Christmas trees in the winter, and a few shrubs in between.'

And Quinn would just bet that they helped each other out at busy times. There was definite camaraderie there. The kind of camaraderie that hadn't really existed between his uncle and aunt and their fellow shopkeepers.

When they'd finished their mugs of tea, they said their goodbyes to Carissa's grandparents and headed for the market. Half the stallholders seemed to know her and greet her with a smile. As they reached the Wyldes' fruit stall, Carissa was enveloped in a bear hug by her uncle George and her cousin Little George; the name was clearly just to distinguish him from his father, because Little George was over six feet tall.

'So you're helping our girl?' George asked.

'Neighbour. Tree-carrying duties,' Quinn said economically.

George clapped him on the back. 'Good lad.'

Three stalls down, Carissa looked at her tree and haggled with Big Jake—who lived up to his name, because he was taller than Little George and twice as broad. Clearly it was all banter and they were both enjoying themselves, Quinn thought, and this was another side to Carissa. A side he liked very much.

Once they'd come to an agreement and had finalised it with a hug, it was Quinn's job to carry the tree back to the car. The scent of pine was strong in his nostrils, sharp and clean.

She'd put the back seat down before driving here so it was easier to load, and he noticed that she'd laid a blanket down so the needles wouldn't spill everywhere in the back of her car. He had to hide a smile; Carissa was so good at organisation and planning that she would've been great working for some of his clients.

'You're quiet,' she said, on the way back.

'Thinking about work,' he fibbed.

She grimaced. 'Sorry, I've taken up too much of your time this morning.'

'No, it's fine. Sometimes it's good to walk away from my desk and let things brew in the back of my mind,' he said. He paused. 'Your uncle and cousin seemed really pleased to see you.'

'Yes—and it was lovely to see them.' She smiled. 'We really need to sort out a family get-together soon. I guess we're all a bit busy at this time of year.'

Mmm, and didn't Quinn know it. Late November onwards was when the corner shop had been full of tins of biscuits and chocolates, and stock had sometimes ended up spilling over into the house when his uncle had been to the cash and carry. Stock that he'd once made the mistake of opening. He hadn't been able to resist the chocolate tree decorations in their shiny paper, and his uncle had been furious.

He pushed the thought away. Not now. He didn't want to think about his family. Or how long it had been since he'd seen them.

'They'll all be there for the Wylde Ward opening, though,' she continued. 'Both sides of my family.

'I guess they remember you being in hospital.'

She nodded. 'My uncles and aunts visited

every single day. They took it in turns to do a shift so my mum and dad weren't on their own, and made sure they had something to eat because they knew my parents were so worried about me and wouldn't be able to think of anything else.'

'That's nice,' he said. 'Supportive.' Not all families were like that. Not many, in his experience. Carissa Wylde had really lucked out.

'Dad always remembered how good they were. The band hadn't made it big at that point, and just before I was born he had been planning to give up the band and get a job—probably teaching music. But his brothers and sisters wouldn't let him. They told him to give it another year and they'd help him out if he was short of money.'

She smiled. 'He never forgot that. So when the Santa song hit number one, he knew what he was going to do with the money as well as setting up the trust fund—he paid off their mortgages and set up college funds for my cousins. He said if they didn't go to college, then they'd have the deposit for a flat and a bit of support for their career.'

The same as he had done, when he'd developed the app that had made his fortune. In the middle of the recession, when the shop had been in trouble, he'd bailed out his aunt and uncle. He'd paid off their overdraft and their mortgage, as well those of his cousins. But unlike Carissa's father he hadn't really done it out of love. He'd done it so he could make sure he'd paid back every single penny they'd ever spent on him and he didn't feel in their debt any more.

In turn, he knew they resented him for doing it because he'd done it quietly, without telling them or making a fuss. He knew he'd made them feel guilty for the way they'd begrudged him as a child. And guilt wasn't a good thing where family was concerned. Sometimes it was easier to sulk in silence than to apologise for past hurts.

Carissa didn't seem to notice that he'd gone quiet again.

'The thing is, if any of them had won the lottery or made it big in business, they would all have done the same as he did—looked after their family, because they all love each other.'

Would his cousins have done that for him? Quinn didn't think so—and he couldn't even remember the last time he'd seen them. Which in turn made him feel uncomfortable and guilty. Maybe he should make more of an effort. Didn't they say that blood was thicker than water? Then again, it worked both ways, and his family didn't make the effort either.

'Your dad,' he said, 'sounds special.'

'The whole family is—on both sides.'

At least she seemed to realise how lucky she was.

'Dad was one of the good guys of rock,' she said. 'He never bothered with the bad-boy stuff of sex and drugs and rock and roll—well, except the music bit,' she added with a grin. 'He was always faithful to my mum. He liked a beer with his mates, but there was never any of this getting totally wrecked and smashing up hotel rooms on tour. It was a kind of a joke that they were called the Wylde Boys but they weren't in the slightest bit wild.'

'Ironic,' he agreed.

Finally they were back at Grove End Mews. Quinn hauled the tree out of her car and carried it up the stairs. 'Where do you want me to take it?' he asked.

'The living room, please.'

Again, trust Carissa to be organised. She had a tub ready and earth to cover the tree's roots. He helped her put the tree in the tub and really hoped that she wasn't going to ask him to help decorate it. Right now he was pretty much Christmassed out.

'The least I can do is to make you some lunch, if you have time,' Carissa said.

Time. That was his perfect excuse.

But again his mouth wasn't playing ball. 'Thanks. I'd like that.'

She made a plate of sandwiches—the softest sourdough bread, filled with sharp cheddar cheese and paired with sweet chilli chutney. Being Carissa, she served it with salad.

'Making sure we get our five a day?' he teased

'Considering you'd try and tell me pizza's a food group,' she teased back.

'That's because it is,' he deadpanned.

'Thanks for coming with me today, Quinn.'

'Pleasure,' he said politely. Even though it had unsettled him slightly.

'I love this bit of Christmas. The scent of a proper tree, then trimming it.'

He'd always hated that bit. They'd had an artificial tree, with thin tinsel that never really sparkled. He could still remember being shouted at when he'd dropped a couple of the glass baubles—they'd shattered, and one of his cousins had stepped on a thin shard of glass and ended up in the emergency department to have it removed. Christmas that year had been one of deep contrition.

She looked at him and sighed. 'You hate all that, don't you?'

'Bah, humbug,' he said, not wanting to tell her any more.

'I won't ask you to help me, then,' she said.

'And please don't present me with a mini decorated tree.' Because it would be just like her to do that.

'You bought me Christmassy fairy lights for my laptop,' she reminded him.

'That's different. Actually, now you've made me think of Project Sparkle,' he said, relieved to change the subject. 'I was going to ask you, how do you choose the projects you get involved with?'

'Sometimes it's something I read in the local paper,' she said. 'Not necessarily my own—I use a cuttings service to pick out things of potential interest.'

'So what you do mostly is fund projects?'

She shook her head. 'Sometimes people need help with organising something or developing a business plan. And there are certain charities I can support on the quiet—music therapy's one of my favourites because it makes me feel connected to my parents.'

'Do you ever do things for, say, families in the armed forces where someone's died or been severely disabled?' he asked.

'Yes. Dad rewrote the last chorus of the Santa song one year.' She sang the lines quietly, '"And if my baby can't be home for

Christmas, then Santa keep my baby safe for me.'"

Quinn remembered that. And it had been top of the charts for weeks.

'All the royalties from that version go to the charity that helps wounded soldiers and their families.' She bit her lip. 'Mum and Dad were going to a benefit gig to play that song when their plane crashed.'

'I'm sorry.' He reached out and squeezed her hand. 'I didn't mean to bring back bad memories for you.'

'I know,' she said softly. 'It's just at this time of year I miss them more than at any other time. The anniversary of the crash is the day of the year when I normally make myself a bit scarce. But this year I'm going to celebrate the day with the opening of the Wylde Ward—I'm going to celebrate their lives and the difference they made to others. It'll make the day better.'

He could see tears in her eyes. And he could also see her blink them back. Carissa wasn't looking for pity, and he wasn't offering it.

He knew what he wanted to offer her. But he also knew that it wouldn't be enough for Carissa, so it was pointless even thinking about it. 'I'd better let you get on with trimming your tree,' he said. 'And I need to be back at my desk.'

'Of course. And thanks for coming with me,' she said.

He was glad that she didn't hug him. Because then he might have done something really stupid—like hugging her back or maybe kissing her. He needed space. Time to remember that he was better off on his own.

Wasn't he?

CHAPTER SEVEN

Magic of Christmas, Proof #3. Up for it or
are you too chicken?

So CARISSA WAS being cheeky now, was she?
Quinn smiled, liking this new aspect of her.
She was funny as well as smart. Where and
when? he texted back.

Your house, 7 p.m. tonight. Don't have
dinner.

He was intrigued, but he knew better than
to bother asking.

At seven, she turned up at his door wearing jeans, a cashmere sweater, a warm jacket
and flat boots.

'So are we going skating again?' he asked.

'Not necessarily,' she said.

Hmm. So skating *could* be on the agenda.

He thought about the time he'd kissed her on the ice, and he went hot all over.

'The reason I'm wearing flat boots is because we're walking there,' she said.

Local, then. Quinn had no idea what she had in mind. And it turned out to be something he hadn't even noticed being set up at the far end of Grove End Park: the Winter Fantasia, a temporary Christmas theme park. There were fairy lights everywhere in the trees—just the kind of thing he already knew Carissa loved, and he could hear Christmassy songs being played in the middle of the park.

'It's not just proof,' she said, as they walked through the park towards the Winter Fantasia. 'I was thinking what you were saying about injured soldiers. Project Sparkle could arrange a trip here for some of the families, with tickets for the rides and what have you.'

'Not everyone likes Christmas,' he reminded her.

'If it works for *you*,' she said, 'then it will work for anyone.'

He winced. 'Ouch. You make me sound like Ebenezer Scrooge.'

She laughed. 'Well, you have to admit you are a bit. Not in a mean way. Just…'

'I don't like Christmas,' he said softly. 'And

I'm not alone. A lot of people don't like the holiday season.'

'And a lot of people do,' she countered. 'This place is fabulous. There's an ice garden with sculptures, a Christmas circus, a fairground and a Christmas market. And a skating rink, though as we've already skated I think we can skip the skating here.'

Pity. He would've liked another excuse to hold her hand. Just to keep him steady on the ice, of course.

She smiled. 'And you'll definitely like the food. Christmas-themed junk food.'

That cheered him up a little bit. 'And we have to do everything here, except the skating?'

'Of course, because, actually, we're multitasking. This is a proof of the magic of Christmas, but it's also a reconnaissance mission for Project Sparkle.'

Only Carissa would manage to make their evening do two things at once.

'OK,' he said. 'On the proof side, what I see is another ker-ching moment. Stalls full of overpriced things that nobody really needs but they buy the stuff anyway because it's this time of year and they feel they ought to.'

'You're telling me you don't like fairgrounds either?' she asked, sounding sceptical.

He couldn't even remember the last time he'd been to a fairground. 'Convince me,' he said.

Carissa was beginning to think that Quinn was impossible.

How could he not see the magic here? Everyone around them was happy and smiling, the whole place felt festive, and the lights and the music were irresistible.

They went on the fairground first—an old-fashioned one with a helter-skelter where you sat on a hessian sack and whizzed round and round. They followed it up with a turn on an old-fashioned carousel with white horses all decked out in tinsel and wearing Santa hats; the fairground organ in the middle of the carousel was playing Christmassy songs. Carissa couldn't help looking at Quinn and grinning when her father's Santa song came on halfway through their turn; he pulled the most gruesome face in return, and they didn't stop laughing until the ride stopped.

She began to relax as he seemed to be enjoying himself. They queued up for the old-fashioned swing boats, where Quinn showed off horrendously, trying to make their boat swing higher than the guy in the swing boat next to them could make his boat go, and Carissa didn't stop laughing through that one either.

On the hook-a-duck stall they were guaranteed a prize and she insisted that Quinn should keep the tiny plastic duck with an improbable Santa hat.

Next was the giant Ferris wheel; it was rather faster-moving than the sedate pace of the London Eye, and it was also open to the elements rather than having completely enclosed cars, so they could feel the chill of the night air against their faces. 'Just look at that,' she said, when they got to the top. 'It's so pretty.' They could see the whole park spread out below them. 'It looks like a fairy tale.'

He coughed. 'Isn't that the whole point of a Winter Fantasia, Carissa? To look like a fairy tale?'

She ignored the Grinchness of his comment. 'The lights make it look as if there's a sprinkle of snow on the trees.' Added to the scents of cinnamon and ginger and vanilla in the air, it was just perfect and she loved it.

Quinn said nothing, and she realised then that he didn't believe in fairy tales, not even deep down.

Who had crushed his belief in magic? she wondered. He never spoke about his family, and he'd gone very quiet after meeting hers.

Maybe like her he'd lost both his parents, but maybe unlike her he hadn't had any support from the rest of his family.

And then there had been that heartfelt comment that she wasn't high maintenance. She had the distinct feeling that someone had broken his heart, and that was why Quinn kept people at a distance. He'd seemed to let her close for that moment on the ice when he'd kissed her—but then he'd gone right back into his shell again.

She knew there was no point in asking him, because he wouldn't tell her. He'd just change the subject or ask her something to distract her. Quinn O'Neill was a very private man.

Although Carissa had sworn never to get involved with anyone after Justin, she found herself drawn to Quinn. He was unlike anyone she'd ever met before. But she had the feeling that he found it as hard to trust as she did. They were both damaged. So they really ought to be sensible about this and stick to being just neighbours and colleagues on Project Sparkle business.

She had to work to suppress the urge to lean over and touch her mouth to his, but she'd managed to get herself back under control by the time their car on the Ferris wheel stopped at the bottom to let them out.

They walked down the avenue together, browsing along more stalls.

Quinn won a coconut on the coconut shy, and presented it to her with a bow.

Then they came to the roller-coaster.

'We don't have to do this one,' Carissa said.

Quinn looked surprised. 'Why not? Are you scared of heights?'

She shook her head. 'Not heights exactly—it's just the bit where you go over the hump at the top and rush downhill. The same as when you go over a hump-backed bridge and your stomach swoops.'

He tsked at her, shaking his head solemnly. 'Now, who was it who called me chicken and said we had to do everything?'

She knew he was only teasing, but at the same time he did have a point. She forced herself to damp down her fear. 'OK. Let's do it.'

'I was kidding,' he said, suddenly looking anxious. 'We can skip it if you'd rather.'

'No. I can do this.' And maybe pushing herself a bit further here physically might help her to be braver when it came to more emotional stuff. Maybe she could learn to put the rest of her fears behind her and start to learn to trust.

As the car creaked slowly up the first hill of the roller-coaster, Carissa felt her skin grow clammy. Just before they reached the top, Quinn took her hand. 'On the count of three, we're going to raise our arms and shout "Christmas",' he told her.

It shocked her into forgetting to be scared.

Was Quinn O'Neill finally seeing the magic?

He still had his fingers laced through hers when he raised his arms, and both of them shouted 'Christmas'. Carissa could feel the rush of adrenalin and the wind in her hair and the fear just melted away. She was still laughing when they got to the bottom of the dip, and this time she didn't feel the full extent of the fear as the car climbed the next slope. She actually enjoyed the rush when they started speeding downhill again, with their arms held up and shouting 'Christmas'.

Somehow Quinn was still holding her hand as they got off the roller-coaster. Carissa didn't want to say anything to break the spell. Right at that moment she felt safe, happy and warm; and she couldn't quite remember the last time she'd felt like this.

They wandered through the garden of ice sculptures, still hand in hand. There was a smiling snowman with a top hat, a Santa and Christmas trees, and a clutch of reindeer with beautiful antlers—and one of them even had a red nose. Following the winter theme, there were penguins and polar bears.

But then they came to a peacock.

'How is a peacock the slightest bit related to Christmas?' Quinn asked. 'Or winter, for that matter? I always think of peacocks wandering round the garden of stately homes in the middle of summer.'

'It's still fabulous,' Carissa said. 'I don't care if it's not strictly Christmassy. Look at the detail of the feathers—they're all fanned out, and there are even eyes carved into the feathers. It's stunning.'

'The sculptors are very talented,' Quinn agreed, 'and I can see a lot of work's gone into this.' He looked at her and raised an eyebrow. 'Are you wishing you'd ordered an ice sculpture instead of a virtual Santa now?'

'As well as, not instead of,' she said, returning his grin. 'But there isn't enough time to do it. I guess they need to plan that sort of thing way in advance so they can freeze big enough blocks of ice to sculpt.' She thought about it. 'Plus not all the kids would be well enough to come outside to see the sculpture and we couldn't take it indoors because it'd melt too quickly. And it'd be a nightmare to clean up all that water.'

'Practical as well as a dreamer,' he said,

sounding approving; it made her feel warm inside.

They headed for the food section next, queuing up for German hot dogs and then sticky Christmas gingerbread.

'You've got sugar on the corner of your mouth,' he said, and skimmed his index finger across her skin.

It was the lightest contact, but it left every nerve-end tingling. And then he kept the eye contact going and licked his finger. A kind of kiss by proxy.

Oh, help.

Because now Carissa really, really wanted him to kiss her. Just like he had at the skating rink.

Quinn's eyes went dark and there was a slash of colour across his cheeks.

Was he remembering the same moment that she was? Did he want to repeat it, too?

She could feel herself tipping her head back slightly, practically offering her mouth to him, and it made her cringe. How pathetic was she? The same weak, stupid woman that had let her boyfriend hit her.

But then, before she could start despising herself again, he moved closer.

'Carissa,' he said softly, and his voice sounded almost rusty.

'Yes.' And she knew he realised she was answering the question he hadn't asked. The question in his eyes.

He rested his hands on her waist and dipped his head, brushing his mouth lightly against hers. 'You taste of sugar and spice,' he said.

'So do you,' she whispered.

And then he did it again.

She was conscious of the song blasting out from the middle of the fairground—'All I Want for Christmas is You'—and she realised at that moment how true the song was. Because all she really wanted for Christmas was Quinn O'Neill.

He kissed her right to the end of the song.

By the time he'd finished she was practically dizzy with need and desire and her knees felt as if they'd turned to mush.

Where did they go from here?

And was she just about to make a really bad mistake, the way she had with Justin? Could she trust her instincts this time?

As if he could see the panic in her eyes, he stroked her cheek. 'I think we have a circus to attend.'

He was letting her off the hook.

For now.

But at least he didn't let her hand go. He kept his fingers entwined with hers all the while they browsed through the Christmas stalls, except for the moments when she was picking up decorations and looking at them before making herself resist them.

And he held her hand all the way through the circus performance—amazing gymnasts on springboards jumping higher and higher and doing more and more complicated somersaults; a juggler; clowns who threw buckets of glitter over the audience and water over each other; a tightrope walker; and daring trapeze artists who timed their leaps to milliseconds. They both found themselves oohing and ahhing with the rest of the audience. But most of all Carissa was aware of the fact that Quinn was still holding her hand.

'So what's the verdict?' she asked as they left the circus.

'Are we talking proof, or are we talking Sparkle business?' he asked.

There had been moments where she'd seen the magic of Christmas reflected in his eyes. And there had definitely been a moment when she'd experienced the magic of Christmas from his lips; but had it been the same for him? Right now she was too chicken to put it to the test and ask him outright. 'Sparkle,' she said.

'I think kids would love it—the rides and

the food. The little ones would love the lights and the ice sculptures. Though some of them might find the clowns scary.'

'Are you telling me you were scared of clowns when you were little?' she teased— and she regretted her words the very next second when she saw his barriers come straight back up and he disentangled his hand from hers. She wished she'd kept her mouth shut. 'Sorry. I wasn't prying,' she said softly.

He gave her a smile that didn't quite reach his eyes. 'I know.'

But it was too late. The moment had been destroyed.

They walked back through the park to Grove End Mews. Carissa didn't quite have the courage to reach for Quinn's hand, because she didn't want him to reject her. And the silence between them had become awkward rather than companionable.

They paused outside her front door.

'Do you, um, want to come in for coffee?' she asked.

'Thanks, but I have stuff I need to be getting on with,' he said.

He'd been polite, but Carissa knew it was just an excuse to save her feelings. She gave him her brightest, glitziest smile. 'Well, thanks for coming with me. I'll catch you later.'

* * *

Quinn knew a brave, fake smile when he saw one—and he felt guilty as hell that he'd pushed Carissa into that role. He knew that her ex had made her do that, too. OK, so he hadn't hurt her physically, the way Justin had done, but he still knew he'd hurt her and he hated himself for that.

But right now he needed some space to let himself think about all this.

It would be, oh, so easy to let himself fall for Carissa Wylde. To fall for the magic that she saw in Christmas—the way she saw the joy in things, the way her smile brightened up a room. And he hadn't been able to resist kissing her in the middle of the Winter Fantasia. Especially with that song playing. Because he'd realised right at that moment that what he really wanted for Christmas was Carissa Wylde.

But.

She'd been hurt in the past. Physically as well as emotionally.

And Quinn didn't think he was the one who could rescue her. Particularly as he knew he'd already been guilty of hurting people who'd wanted more from him emotionally than he'd been prepared to give. He could still see the look on Janine's face when he'd told her it just wasn't working and he didn't want to mess her about—it was his fault, not hers, but they needed to break up. The light in her eyes had just drained away, and she'd looked crushed. He didn't want to hurt Carissa like that, too. But he didn't know how to change.

He let himself into his own house, miserable and wishing now that he'd made an excuse not to go with her. Because he'd lied to her, too. He'd deliberately made her think that he was being all bah-humbuggy, when this time he'd seen the magic. Felt it in the touch of her hand, the warmth of her skin against his.

He knew what he wanted for Christmas all right.

But, just like through all his childhood years, he knew he wasn't going to get it. So it was pointless wishing.

CHAPTER EIGHT

SHOULD HE GIVE Carissa the present in person, or should he just post it through her letterbox?

Quinn stared at the Christmas-tree decoration.

He'd seen it on one of the stalls last night, but there had been no way at the time he could have bought it as a surprise for Carissa. Not without either letting go of her hand—and he'd discovered that he really, really liked strolling hand in hand with Carissa Wylde—or making some excuse to double back to the stall without her. There hadn't been the right moment.

Fortunately the peacock hadn't been sold between last night and the time when Winter Fantasia had opened this morning, so he'd been able to buy it this morning—a glittery confection of turquoise and gold with its little crown and spread-out feathers.

If he gave the ornament to Carissa in person, there was a good chance she might think there were strings attached. He'd bought it simply because he'd thought she might enjoy it. Like the fairy lights for her laptop—though admittedly those had been for a purpose. To persuade her to answer his questions about Project Sparkle. The peacock was simply to make her smile.

And he probably needed his head examined.

In the end, he scribbled the word 'Enjoy' on the top sheet of the jotter block on his desk, signed it with his initial, put the note and the unwrapped peacock into a padded envelope, and scrawled her name on the front.

He was pretty sure it was an office day for her, so he simply posted the package through her letterbox—it was just thin enough to fit—and then headed back to his desk, to work on the app he'd been tinkering with all week. At least if he buried himself in work he could concentrate and stop thinking about her, he told himself.

And he knew he was lying.

Carissa came home from a busy day at the office to find a pile of post on her doormat when she unlocked the front door. Christmas cards, a couple of brochures, a bank statement—and a padded envelope that just had her name written on the front. Clearly it had been delivered by hand, by someone who knew where she lived. And the padded bag had obviously been reused, because the front was rough where an adhesive label had been removed.

She didn't recognise the handwriting. Curious, she opened the envelope and discovered a beautiful glittery peacock. A Christmas-tree ornament with a little loop to let it hang from a branch.

Who was it from?

She looked inside the bag again and discovered the note. Not exactly verbose: just the word 'Enjoy', and it was signed with a single initial.

Q.

Quinn.

He'd bought her a peacock for her tree. A reminder of last night, when she'd fallen for the ice sculpture?

A reminder of last night, when he'd held her hand and kissed her?

And then all his barriers had come back up because she'd said the wrong words at the wrong time.

She couldn't quite work him out. So what now? Was this his version of an olive branch, a way of reopening communications between them after he'd gone all closed off on her?

There was only one way to find out.

She called him, but his phone went straight through to voice mail. Maybe he didn't want to talk to her after all; or maybe he was just busy. Rather than leaving a message, she texted him a brief thank-you note.

Carissa had just finished putting the peacock on the tree and her cards on the ribbon where she displayed them when her phone rang.

'Hello,' Quinn said.

'Hello.' She paused. 'Thank you for the peacock. It's fabulous.'

'My pleasure.'

She waited. What now?

'I, um, enjoyed yesterday,' he said.

Which bit? She just about stopped herself from asking him the question. Too needy. Too pathetic. 'So did I,' she said. She went to the Fantasia every year with friends and always enjoyed it, but last night had been different. Special.

There was another slightly awkward pause, and then he said, 'Do you want to come over and watch a movie?'

Was he asking her on a kind of date, or was he just being neighbourly?

'What kind of movie?' she asked.

'*Not* a Christmas one.' There was a hint of amusement in his voice. 'Though I don't mind whether it's a comedy, an action movie or a thriller. Maybe we can choose when you get here?'

'I'll bring popcorn,' she said. 'Give me five minutes.'

Quinn felt like a teenager.

Which was totally ridiculous.

He was thirty years old—not a shy, spotty thirteen-year-old who was too nervous to ask out the girl of his dreams in case she said no and everyone at school found out and laughed at him.

Nobody laughed at him, he didn't have spots, and he was always the one to say no—he'd turned down quite a few offers. But he still felt like that nervous thirteen-year-old.

In five minutes—with typical lawyerly precision—Carissa rang his doorbell. Thankfully she wasn't wearing her unapproachable lawyer suit, but the long-sleeved silky T-shirt she wore clung in all the right places and rendered Quinn temporarily tongue-tied.

He just about remembered his manners enough to offer her a drink.

Then she handed him a sealed paper bag. 'I'm assuming you have a microwave.'

He gave her a look. 'Not all of us have the

time or the inclination to whip up a gourmet six-course meal in three seconds flat.'

'Six courses is just greedy, and you're totally exaggerating the time.' She laughed. 'So shut up and stick that in the microwave for three minutes.'

He couldn't help laughing back and, following her instructions, he let the microwave pop in the bag while he poured them both a glass of wine, then ushered her into his sitting room.

Hot, buttery popcorn and crisp Pinot Grigio: it was a good combination.

The only thing that could make it better, Quinn thought, would be if he scooped her on to his lap. But the last time he'd done that had been when she'd told him about Justin. He didn't want to bring back bad memories for her, so for now he'd be content just to sit next to her on the sofa.

'Want to choose the movie?' he asked, flicking into the film app and then handing her the remote control for the television.

She smiled at him 'Are you quite sure I can't pick a Christmas one?'

'Quite sure,' he said.

'Pity,' she said, 'because *It's a Wonderful Life* is the best movie ever.'

He didn't care. He didn't want all the gooey Christmassy stuff shoved down his throat.

'Maybe you need your own personal Clarence,' she said.

He rather thought his Clarence might be female, though her name was very similar to that of the angel in the movie. 'Hmm,' he said.

'OK. How about a rom-com?' she tested.

He was happy to put up with something sappy if it meant sitting on the sofa with her. 'Anything you like—' he began.

'As long as it's not a Christmas movie,' she finished with a grin.

In the end she picked a comedy that was a little bit too slapstick for his sense of humour—but it was amusing enough. Somehow, he ended up holding her hand, and to his relief she returned the pressure of his fingers.

And when they'd finished the popcorn and he'd put the bowl on the floor out of the way, it was easy just to shift position slightly, so she had to lean against him. Which meant that it was easier still to move so that she was properly in his arms. They ended up lying full length on the sofa, with her head pillowed on his shoulder and his arms wrapped round her waist.

He could put up with the movie a lot more easily after that.

At the end of the movie she said, 'I really enjoyed that.'

'Mmm.' He'd been much more focused on the pleasure of just holding her.

She turned to face him and laid her palm against his face. 'Are you still working on that surveillance stuff?'

'Why?'

'I'm not prying—I know your work is confidential and I wouldn't dream of asking you to break any rules,' she said. 'But do you remember we talked about a surveillance system for a house?'

'And you said you'd think about it. Obviously you have.' He held her gaze. 'So are we talking about your house, Carissa?'

'No.'

Clearly she wasn't going to tell him any more than that. Which really didn't help.

'I can build you a system,' he said, 'but I would have to see the house first. I can't work blind. I need to look at the house and its surroundings, so I can tell where the problem areas are. And it won't just be me on the team. My expertise is the system itself, but I'd need a colleague to help survey the house and its grounds.'

She looked thoughtful. For a minute he thought she was going to back off again, but then she nodded. 'OK, but only if your colleague is female.'

He frowned.

She paused. 'There is a reason for it.'

'Which is?'

'A good reason.'

Another of her non-answers. 'Are you going to tell me?'

'Um—not right now.'

'You really have trust issues, don't you?' he asked.

'That's a bit pots and kettles,' she said, 'considering that you don't trust anyone either.' She wriggled out of his arms and sat up. 'Is it to do with the woman who hurt you?'

'I have no idea what you're talking about,' he said frostily, also sitting up and folding his arms.

'Yes, you do. The one you said was high maintenance.'

How had he let himself forget that she was a lawyer? Carissa paid attention to details and she remembered things. It was her job—but it was also who she was. The woman who laid a table properly, with damask tablecloths and napkins, and used serving platters even for takeaway pizza.

'That's in the past and it's staying there,' he said.

'No, it's not,' she said, 'because it's stopping you moving forward.'

He narrowed his eyes at her. 'You mean like you and Justin?'

He'd expected her to get angry with him. Instead, she just looked sad. 'Exactly like me and Justin. Though at least I'm trying to move on from my past.'

Meaning that he wasn't? Though maybe she had a point. He'd dated, since Tabitha—quite a lot—but every single one of his girlfriends had complained that he was too distant. And he'd compounded that by almost never having more than three dates with the same person, not wanting to risk getting hurt. He sighed and closed his eyes. 'It's like I said to you before. Sometimes you just pick the wrong person.'

And then he felt her fingers curling round his. 'You also said,' she reminded him softly, 'that it was OK to walk away. Is that what you did?'

He'd never really talked about Tabitha to anyone. And although he hadn't meant to say another syllable on the subject, he found the words spilling out. 'No. She was the one who walked away.'

'You loved her more than she loved you.' It was a statement rather than a question. No pity, no contempt, just acceptance. Because she'd been there, too.

'I wasn't what she wanted. I wasn't enough for her.' He looked straight at Carissa.

She said nothing, simply waiting for him to talk—just like he'd waited for her to tell him about Justin.

Fair was fair.

He'd kept her confidence and he knew without having to ask that she would keep his, because Carissa Wylde had the biggest heart in the world.

'I met Tabitha at a party. A friend of a friend of a friend.' He hadn't really dated that much before then, concentrating on his career and being the best he could possibly be. Playing second fiddle to his work hadn't gone down that well with his girlfriends. But his friends had talked him into loosening up a bit and going to that fateful party. He hadn't been on the receiving end of charm like Tabitha's before, and he'd fallen for her hook, line and sinker.

He gave Carissa a mirthless smile. 'I'd just graduated and I'd been headhunted to work for…a government department. And I think she liked the idea of having a geeky boyfriend with those kinds of connections.'

'Clever being the new sexy,' she said softly.

'Or something like that. She was gorgeous. And way out of my league.'

Carissa raised her eyebrows. 'Have you looked in a mirror lately?'

'Thank you for the compliment, but I wasn't fishing.'

'I know.'

'I meant socially,' he said. 'I came from a different background. I didn't fit in with her friends or her family. I was stupid enough to think that it didn't matter—I loved her and she loved me, so of course it would all work out.' What he'd loved more had been the idea of having a family—people who'd accept him for who he was and maybe even love him back. And he'd been young enough to be really, really hurt when it had turned out to be the opposite.

Carissa's fingers tightened round his. 'That's not stupid at all. In a relationship, you both make compromises. My parents came from different backgrounds, and it was never an issue.'

'Because your parents loved each other,' he said. 'That was my big mistake. Tabitha didn't love me.' He blew out a breath. 'I spent Christmas at her family's home, that year. It was awful. I didn't have the right clothes with me. I didn't get any of their traditions. Half the time I wasn't even sure that we were speaking the same language—I certainly didn't get their in-jokes or their pet names.'

'That was incredibly rude of them,' Carissa said. 'If you invite someone to stay at your home, then you make them *feel* at home. You don't exclude them. And if there's a dress code, you tell people well in advance.'

'To be fair to them, I probably didn't try hard enough,' Quinn said.

Carissa scoffed. 'You're supposed to make a fuss of your guests. And that has nothing to do with social class and everything to do with common good manners.' She paused. 'I'm assuming you broke up with her at Christmas, so that's another strike against Christmas for you?'

'No,' he said. 'I overheard a conversation between Tabitha and her sister. It should have warned me that it was time to end things—her sister said that Tabitha was dating me just to rebel against her parents.'

'Tabitha,' Carissa said crisply, 'needed to grow up. A lot.'

'She was twenty. A year younger than me.'

Carissa's expression said very clearly, *My point exactly.*

'We survived Christmas,' he said. 'But not for much longer. I must've made some comment that made her think I was going to do something stupid, like suggest moving in together. She picked a fight with me, and then she told me that she was just using me to rebel against her parents because I was so different from her family and friends. And I'd been naive enough to think that although she'd started dating me because I was a geek, she'd grown to like me for who I was.' He shrugged. 'Learned that one the hard way.'

'Quinn, you were twenty-one. Still a baby, really. You made a mistake, and that's fine— that's how you learn. But I think you took the wrong lessons away. Because you,' Carissa said, 'are worth much more than being someone's rebellion.'

And Carissa was worth much more than being some City brat's punchbag. Not that he was going to bring that up. He'd find a nicer way to tell her.

'For the record,' she said, 'your background and your accent and the way you dress don't matter. It's who you are, how you treat other people and whether you have a good heart that counts.'

He wasn't so sure that he had a good heart. Just a damaged one. Because after Tabitha he hadn't wanted to risk getting hurt again—trying too hard and getting it wrong. He'd gone too far the other way, but he just couldn't work out a middle ground. 'A good heart,' he repeated.

Her fingers tightened round his. 'And it sounds to me as if Ms High Maintenance didn't have one.'

'Maybe,' he said. Or maybe just not the right one for him.

'You fit in around here,' she pointed out.

He'd noticed that people raised a hand to him across the courtyard, or nodded to him from their cars. Though Carissa was the only one who'd gone further than that. And, given what she did with Project Sparkle, he thought she might have a habit of taking in waifs and strays. Was he part of that?

'The house…it's a safe house,' she said suddenly, surprising him.

She had his full attention now. 'For people trying to leave a violent home, you mean?'

She nodded. 'Women and children.'

Had she used the safe house when she'd left Justin?

He didn't want to make her feel bad by asking.

But he remembered that when she'd talked about it, she'd said something about making amends for not taking her ex to court. This was obviously what she meant. Being involved with a safe house.

And now he knew why she wanted him to bring a female colleague. So the people in the safe house continued feeling safe.

'I do have a female colleague I can ask to do the survey with me,' he said. 'Are you sure people wouldn't mind me being there?'

'It's fine—because you'll be there with me.'

So did that mean she trusted him?

Or maybe she trusted him as much as she dared to trust anyone outside her immediate family.

'Do you volunteer there?' he asked softly.

'Sort of,' she said. 'Although my day job's mainly in contract law, I know enough about family law to help sort out injunctions when they're needed.'

And he'd just bet she didn't charge a penny for her work either. That would be her way of making amends for not taking Justin to court.

'That's good,' he said softly.

She was still holding his hand.

He brought her fingers up to his mouth and kissed each knuckle in turn. 'You have a good heart.'

'I have a good family. I learned from them.'

It would be easy to let her draw him into talking about his family. But he'd already gone far enough for now, talking about Tabitha. He didn't want to dump the rest of his baggage on her. 'That's good,' he said, meaning it. 'I'll talk to my colleague tomorrow.'

'Thank you,' she said quietly. 'And I'm not asking for a freebie. I'll pay the going rate.'

'Payback?' he asked softly.

'What goes around comes around. I was lucky. I had people there for me. Not everyone's that fortunate.' She looked away. 'And I guess I'd better head for home. I'm due in the office tomorrow, and you're busy.'

'Yeah.' Work was his favourite excuse. But he was beginning to rethink it.

'I loved the peacock. And the movie. Thank you.' She dropped a swift kiss on the corner of his mouth. 'I'll talk to you later.'

He nearly asked her to stay.

Nearly.

But he didn't think either of them was quite ready for that.

'Later,' he said, and walked her back to her front door. Just because he was a little bit old-fashioned and it made him feel happier to know she was home safely. And she clearly knew it, because she let him walk her home.

'Goodnight, Quinn,' she said softly.

'Goodnight, Carissa. Sweet dreams.' And he knew his own would be sweet. Because they'd be of her.

CHAPTER NINE

'THANK YOU,' CARISSA said in the car on the way back to Grove End Mews from the safe house.

Quinn shrugged. 'You asked me to bring a female colleague to help with the survey. Mara's good at her job. She pays attention to detail.'

Like Carissa herself. But Quinn had been really, really quiet ever since they'd visited the refuge.

'I'm not trying to pry,' she said. 'I'm just trying to apologise in case I've trodden on a sore spot.'

He frowned. 'How do you mean?'

'If you knew someone who...' Her voice trailed off. There wasn't a tactful way to phrase it.

'Are you asking me if I've been in a safe house before?'

'Um—yes,' she admitted.

'No,' he said. 'I haven't.'

'OK.' She needed to learn to shut up. Saying too much had always been the quickest way to make Justin's temper boil over.

As if he'd heard a wobble in her voice and guessed what was behind it, Quinn reached over and squeezed her hand. 'I'm not saying much because I found that place a bit—well— shocking. Seeing the fear in the eyes of the women and children. Worse still, the way they masked that fear so quickly, as if showing fear would make someone attack them.' He blew out a breath. 'Was that what it was like for you?'

She had to swallow hard because of the lump in her throat. 'Yes.'

'Right now,' he said, 'I feel utterly ashamed of my gender.'

'That's not fair. You're not like Justin. You're not like the men who hit women.'

'I hope not.'

That sounded heartfelt. She could understand why he felt so bad. It wasn't nice, facing up to the dark side of other people. Right now, she thought he needed something to make him feel better. And she knew just the thing. 'Quinn—can we do something tonight? Something nice? I know you hate Christmas, but…'

'If it's something that makes me feel clean again, then yes,' he said. 'Even if it's one of your spurious proofs of a magic we both know doesn't exist.'

Clean.

A vision of him flashed into her mind. In the shower. With her.

Oh, help.

And what she'd just said sounded tantamount to asking him out on a date.

She wouldn't be surprised if he backed away.

And yet he'd said yes. He wanted to do something nice with her.

'OK,' she said. 'I just need to check some times.' Even though she knew she was being a bit of a coward, using her phone as a barrier to keep a little distance between them.

When he parked outside his house, she climbed out of the car. 'I'll see you at mine, at six-thirty?'

'Sure.'

'And thanks again, Quinn. And I want you to bill me for all the work you and Mara do. All the equipment, too.'

'Uh-huh,' he said.

Carissa spent the rest of the day working on Project Sparkle ideas, grabbed a quick sandwich, then changed into slightly smarter clothing that was more appropriate for what they were doing that evening.

But Quinn wasn't there at six-thirty. Or ten minutes later.

She'd already worked out that Quinn was punctual. So had he changed his mind?

Just to check, she texted him. Still on for a Magic of Christmas thing?

Thirty seconds later, her phone rang. 'Carissa, I'm so sorry,' Quinn said. 'I completely lost track of time.'

Then she felt guilty. He was busy at work, and she'd already taken up quite enough of his time today on the surveillance project for the refuge. 'Look—we don't have to do this.'

'Yes, we do. Give me five minutes to save my file and sort a couple of things out,' he said.

It was more like fifteen, but at least he turned up. Odd how much that warmed her.

'So what are we doing?' he asked.

'I'm having a bit of a panic now,' she said, 'because now I've thought about it I realise you're probably going to hate it—but it's something that always makes me feel better.'

'As long as it doesn't involve more Z-list celebs switching on lights, that's fine,' he said. Though the smile most definitely reached his eyes.

'We're walking,' she said. 'Though we might not get a seat.'

She took him through Grove End Park

to St Mary's, a gothic-looking church made from sand-coloured stone. Inside were cream-painted soaring arches, dark wooden pews, Victorian stained glass and a pale marble floor. Instead of having the electric chandeliers blazing out, the church was lit by tiny tealight candles placed on the little ledge on the back of each pew. There was a tall Christmas tree next to the pulpit, decked out with what looked like decorations made especially by the children in the local nursery schools, with a silver star at the top. The sharp, clean scent of the fir tree filled the church. The benches for the choir were full, with the adult members at the back, all dressed in turquoise robes, and the children standing at the front, wearing white chorister robes.

Because Carissa and Quinn had arrived only just in time for the start of the service, they had to stand at the back rather than sit in the pews, but she didn't mind. It was the atmosphere she'd wanted. Calm and sweet and full of love.

'A carol service?' Quinn whispered.

'Yes. I always used to do this with my parents,' she said. 'Don't worry. You don't have to sing if you don't want to.'

Though she sang along with her favourite carols, 'The Angel Gabriel' and 'Joy to the

World'. As always, the children singing 'Away in a Manger' on their own, and then the child singing a solo in 'Once in Royal David's City', brought tears to her eyes. Just as she blinked the tears back she felt Quinn's fingers twine with hers. Had it touched him, too? She didn't quite dare to look at him.

Afterwards, they filed out of the church. Quinn was still holding her hand.

'Let's not go back just yet,' Quinn said. 'Is there anywhere around here that does hot chocolate?'

'With marshmallows on the top,' she said. 'There is indeed.'

She took him to the small café nearby, where they ordered hot chocolate and mince pies.

'I can't remember the last time I went to a carol service,' Quinn said. 'Probably not since I was at infant school.'

'Sorry,' she said. 'I should have said what I had in mind and given you the chance to say no.'

'I probably would have done,' he admitted, 'but I'm glad you took me.'

Something in his expression stopped her from teasing him about finally seeing the magic of Christmas. This was too important. A breakthrough. Quinn actually trusting her. Given that he'd had his heart stomped on by someone who'd been using him, she could understand why he was so wary of relationships. The fact that he seemed less guarded with her now...that was a good thing. 'I love the candlelit service,' she said. 'It makes me feel connected to centuries of history, people doing the same thing every single year at this time.'

He nodded. 'And it made me feel clean again. Thank you.'

She reached across the table and squeezed his hand. 'Me, too—sometimes life can be a bit dark, but there's still a lot of good stuff out there.'

He didn't pull away, so she carried on holding his hand across the table.

This wasn't officially a date—but it was definitely starting to feel like one.

'You have a lovely voice,' he said.

She smiled. 'Thanks, but I'm not up to Dad's standard.'

'You were in tune and in time when you were singing the carols—not everyone in the congregation was,' he pointed out.

'But they don't have to be,' she said. 'It's about sharing. Being together.'

'I guess.' This time he did pull his hand away.

Carissa had no idea what sore spot she'd clearly just trampled on—something else

Tabitha had done to hurt him? But she knew that if she asked he wouldn't tell her, so instead she took refuge in her hot chocolate and mince pie.

'So what's the current Sparkle project?' he asked. 'Apart from the virtual Santa?'

'Christmas for the safe house,' she said. 'Nothing big and flashy, because they've already had so much to deal with—I don't want to overwhelm anyone or make it look as if I'm trying to buy them happiness. I just want to give them some space to start rebuilding their lives and give them a bit of fun, so they have some good moments to help them deal with the hard stuff.'

'Do you need another virtual Santa?'

She shook her head. 'Anna, who runs the place, has given me some ideas about what everyone would like.

'Well, if you need a hand wrapping stuff,' he said, 'you know where I am.'

She smiled at him. 'I might take you up on that.'

When they'd finished their hot chocolate they walked home through the park. Halfway home, Quinn slid his arm round Carissa's shoulders, and she slid her arm round his waist.

There was frost glittering on the ground,

and Christmas lights in the windows of houses overlooking the park. What with that, the carol service and the hot chocolate, the evening was just perfect, she thought.

At least this time the silence between them was relaxed rather than awkward. Though she still didn't know where this thing between them was going. Clearly there were similarities between her and his high-maintenance ex that made him wary, and she was still trying to get her trust back after Justin, but if they kept it slow and steady, like this, maybe they'd manage to work it out without reopening their scars.

There was one last thing that would make him feel a lot better, Quinn thought. So he made an appointment to see Justin Vaughan. It was possibly a bit mean of him to make it sound as if it was a headhunting opportunity when it was nothing of the sort, but if he told Vaughan the real reason he wanted to talk then he knew that the other man wouldn't turn up.

Vaughan came breezing into the café at the time they'd arranged, all urbane and charming. He looked around, clearly trying to work out which of the other customers was Quinn.

Quinn had just about resisted the temptation to say that he'd be the man with a carnation

in his buttonhole and carrying a copy of the
Financial Times; as he was the 'headhunter',
it was obvious that he'd know what Vaughan
looked like.

He raised his hand, and Vaughan came
over—like an over-eager puppy, except Quinn
rather thought that Vaughan was the type of
man who'd kick an over-eager puppy who got
in his way.

'Mr O'Neill?' Vaughan asked.

'Yes.' He didn't take up Vaughan's offer to
shake his hand. 'Shall we take a walk in the
park for our talk?'

'Ah, confidentiality,' Vaughan said.

Yes, but not in the way Vaughan was thinking. Quinn inclined his head.

He said nothing until they'd crossed the road
and were in the middle of the park. Just as he'd
expected, Vaughan was the one to crack.

'So—you have a job opportunity?' Vaughan
asked.

'An opportunity,' Quinn said carefully.

'What sort of opportunity?'

Quinn stopped and looked Vaughan straight
in the eye. 'An opportunity,' he said, 'to make
some amends.'

'Amends?' Vaughan frowned. 'I don't have
a clue what you're talking about.'

'Breaking a woman's arm,' Quinn said, 'and

not letting her go to the hospital because you knew people would ask questions and the truth would come out.'

Vaughan went white. 'I don't know what you mean.'

'Oh, I rather think you do,' Quinn said softly.

'Who are you? Why are you here?'

'You already know my name. I'm here because of what happened to Carissa. I can't stand by and know that's going to happen to someone else because you can't control your temper.'

'She's lying,' Vaughan blustered.

Quinn raised an eyebrow. 'And you'd be prepared to take an official lie-detector test on that subject, would you?'

'You can't do that.'

'Not personally—but I work with agencies that can.' Quinn smiled thinly. 'And I can assure you that their evidence would stand up in court.'

'What do you want from me?'

'I want you to get some proper counselling,' Quinn said. 'So you learn to deal with whatever it is that makes you hit women, and so that you never even raise your voice in anger to a woman or a child again, let alone hurt them.'

Vaughan lifted his chin in a show of bravado. 'And if I don't?'

It wasn't much of a threat. Quinn could tell that Vaughan was the type who only hit people who couldn't hit back. Quinn was taller, slightly broader, and definitely fitter. Vaughan wouldn't take the risk that he'd come off substantially worse in a fight.

Quinn stared at him. 'I could break every single bone in your body,' he said softly—and calmly enough to make sure that Vaughan realised it wasn't an empty threat, 'but violence doesn't actually solve problems. You'll still be a man who hits vulnerable people. All that would happen is that you'd be temporarily incapacitated. That's not enough.'

'Are you threatening me?'

'No. I'm just telling you that if you hit someone again I'll make sure that the evidence lands on important desks. I don't think your employer would be too keen to have their name associated with a court case. Plus you'd be looking at a prison sentence for actual bodily harm—and I believe they don't take too kindly in prison to men who hit women and children.'

'She wouldn't take me to court,' Vaughan said, relieved. 'She won't want her name in the press. She won't want to embarrass her family.'

'But her family,' Quinn said softly, 'loves

her to bits. And they'll back her all the way. Blackmail isn't nice.'

'Isn't that what you're doing to me?' Vaughan asked.

'No. I'm giving you the choice of sorting yourself out, so the people in your life don't have to spend their lives terrified that they'll say the wrong thing and you'll lash out and hurt them. You can choose to do that; or you can choose to face the legal consequences of your behaviour. Simple, really. All you have to do is the right thing.'

Vaughan just stared at him.

'And I'll know if you don't,' Quinn added. 'Because I'll be watching you.'

It wasn't an empty threat. And Vaughan clearly recognised that, because he gave a defeated nod.

'Good.' Quinn paused. 'Merry Christmas.'

And he walked away, feeling much lighter in spirit. Justin Vaughan was a bully and a coward—but he'd be too afraid of losing his job or ending up in prison to carry on as he was. He'd get help. And what had happened to Carissa wouldn't happen to anyone else.

Two days before opening of the Wylde Ward, Quinn and Mara had sorted out the security system at the safe house and tweaked things to make it safer.

'I need to settle up with you,' Carissa said, and brandished her bank card at him. 'I want an invoice, your bank sort code and account number, and I'll do a direct transfer.'

'I don't feel comfortable charging you for the system,' Quinn said. 'And as I run my own business I can write things off as charitable donations. I'm very happy to do that in this case.'

Carissa shook her head. 'That wasn't the deal—and if you do that, then I can't ask you for help the next time I need something done for Project Sparkle.'

He shrugged. 'Quinn O'Neill, computer geek. Will work for brownies if they're made by Carissa Wylde.' He pursed his lips. 'Or her grandmother. He's not fussy.'

Her eyes crinkled at the corners. 'That's very sweet. And flattering. But, no, Quinn. If nothing else, you have Mara's time and expertise to pay for. And the stuff you bought for the surveillance system. I need to pay you.'

'How about we compromise,' Quinn suggested, 'and I let you pay for Mara's time?'

'*And* the hardware.'

He could see that she wasn't going to budge

on this. 'OK. Do you want to make yourself a coffee while I sort out the costings?'

'Was that Quinn-speak for will I make you a coffee, too?'

He smiled. 'That would be nice.'

By the time she'd finished making the coffee, he'd sorted out the bill.

She scrutinised it—he knew she suspected that he'd undercharged her, rather than thinking that he was trying to rip her off—but eventually she nodded. 'OK. The money will be in your account first thing tomorrow.'

'Thank you.'

'And then,' she said, 'there's our wager. About the virtual Santa.'

'Uh-huh.'

'Double or quits.' She paused. 'So, do you see the magic of Christmas?'

No. He didn't. There had been places where he had—but he rather thought that had more to do with Carissa herself rather than Christmas.

'I think,' he said carefully, 'it's complicated.'

She narrowed her eyes at him. 'OK. I get that bits of it are over-commercialised and there's too much greed. I know you hated the Christmas lights. But you liked the skating.'

'The skating was to do with the fact that it's winter and not with Christmas,' he said. 'If you were in Australia, you'd be skating in

July.' Though he had definitely seen the magic there. When he'd kissed her.

'And you liked the Fantasia.'

'But not because of it being Christmas. I liked the fairground. Fairs happen all year round.'

'You bought me a peacock decoration for my tree,' she pointed out.

'Peacocks,' he reminded her, 'are not Christmassy.'

'Oh, yes, they are—in medieval times, they were Christmas dinner,' she said.

He scoffed. 'Yeah, right.'

'For the nobility,' she said. 'I looked it up. Richard II served peacock to ten thousand people at Warwick Castle for Christmas dinner, as part of a feast that lasted for five days. Apparently they were roasted without the skin and the feathers, then when they were cooked they were sewn back into their skins, their beaks were painted with gilt, and they were served on a platter with their tails fanned out.'

'Sounds like a recipe for food poisoning,' he said with a grimace.

'Maybe.' She paused. 'And there was the carol concert. You said you liked that.'

But most of all he'd enjoyed being with her. 'It's complicated,' he said again.

She put her hands on her hips and stared

narrowly at him. 'So you *do* see it, but you just can't admit it because you're stubborn.'

He sighed. 'No. I just don't like Christmas. I probably never will.'

'Was it that bad when you were little?' she asked.

He felt the panic seep through him. Had he said something indiscreet? 'I'm not sure what you mean,' he prevaricated.

'When people really hate something, it's usually because it has bad memories for them,' she said, 'and that usually dates back to when they were little.'

'You're quite the psychologist,' he said.

She sighed. 'Quinn, every time I think we're getting to know each other, you clam up on me.'

Busted. He couldn't think of anything to say to that, because he knew it was true. So he didn't say anything.

She frowned. 'I just wish…'

'What?'

'Never mind.'

'Now who's clamming up?'

She shook her head. 'OK. You win. I'll pay you double for the virtual Santa.'

He backtracked swiftly. 'No. It's a charitable donation.'

'A charitable donation of a virtual Santa, from someone who hates Christmas.'

'From someone who hates Christmas,' he said, 'but who can still see the good that other people are doing and appreciate that. And I'll be there on the day.' Because he knew how important the day was to her and he wanted to be there for her—but he didn't want to admit that. So he added swiftly, 'You know what systems are like. They crash when you really need them to work properly. It makes sense for me to be there to fix stuff if it's needed.'

'Your systems,' she said, 'apparently work without glitches. It's not going to crash.'

'And you've just tempted fate to make it crash badly,' he said. 'I'll be there.'

'OK. And thank you.' She bit her lip. 'You have a good heart, Quinn. I just wish you'd realise that.'

Maybe he had. Maybe he did. But deep down he knew he wouldn't be enough for Carissa, so once the ward opening day was over he'd back off, very quietly, and let her get on with her life.

CHAPTER TEN

THE NINETEENTH OF December.

The day when Carissa always tried to be brave, to celebrate the wonderful life she'd been able to share with her parents until she was fifteen—until her father's plane had crashed on the way to a charity gig, killing him and her mother and leaving Carissa orphaned.

The day that was always a gaping hole in her life, when the world had no colour or sparkle and it felt as if her shoulders were weighed down by a million sorrows.

And she knew it was as hard for the rest of their family. Not that any of them regretted a moment of the lives of Peter and Isobel Wylde: the regrets were for the time they hadn't had together, for the milestones they'd missed sharing.

'Smile,' she told herself as she picked up the bunch of white roses she always took to her parents' grave on the anniversary of their deaths. 'You're celebrating their lives today. The Wylde Ward is finally opening. You're going to do them proud.'

She walked into the churchyard, took the previous week's flowers out of the vase, topped up the water and threaded the stems of the roses through the little holes in the vase.

'I miss you,' she said. 'I miss you so much. I wish you were here today to see what you've achieved—that the ward you wanted to build for the hospital to thank them for saving me is finally going to be opened today. I wish you were here to play the Santa song, Dad, and get everyone to sing along with you. And I wish you were here to watch him, Mum, with all that love in your face.'

But it wasn't to be.

She blew out a breath.

'And right now I could do with a bit of advice,' she said. 'I've spent three years keeping men at arm's length because I was such an idiot over Justin, and I can't trust myself to pick someone who won't treat me the way he did. And now I've met Quinn. He's special.' She bit her lip. 'I think you would've liked him. Nan and Poppy like him. Granny and Gramps will meet him today, and I'm pretty sure they'll like him, too.'

There was a 'but'.

'But I think he's been badly hurt in the past. He keeps his emotions all wrapped up. Sometimes he just closes off on me. And I don't know if I'm going to be enough to make him change that. I don't know if he'll ever open up to me.' She finished arranging the roses. 'Maybe it's time I took a risk. He's been so brilliant over the virtual Santa. Maybe today of all days he'll let me in.'

But she was pretty sure that he wouldn't.

'I love you,' she said softly. 'I wish you were here. I know you're in me, but I wish you were here so I could hug you both and you'd talk back to me. Which is really selfish, because I have the most brilliant family in the world, and your parents and your brothers and sisters have always been there for me.

'But I so wish you were here. I wish you could meet Quinn. I wish…I just wish we'd had more time together. That you could be there on my wedding day, and on the day when your first grandchild is born.' She sighed. 'Not that I even know if I'm ever going to get married and have children. I'd like to, but I don't know how Quinn feels about me—I don't know if he feels the same way, and I don't know if he wants marriage and children. And now I'm being selfish and maudlin and it's your special day, so I'm just going to shut up and get on with it. But I miss you. I really, really miss you.'

She stroked the top of the headstone, then headed back to Grove End Mews, knowing that she had a hundred and one last-minute things to do for the opening of the ward. She'd already printed her list out in order of priority, and she started ticking her way through it as soon as she got home.

Quinn called round. 'I guess we need to go to the hospital and finish setting up. I want to do a test once we have the system working, to make sure there aren't any bugs. Are you ready?'

No. She was filled with panic. But you were supposed to fake it until you make it, she knew, so she forced herself to smile. 'Ready.'

He took her hand and squeezed it. 'Your parents would be so proud of you.'

'Uh-huh.' Carissa couldn't quite trust herself to speak, because the emotions welled up and blocked her throat.

Quinn drove them to the hospital. The radio was playing Christmas songs but he didn't switch it to something else. Maybe he was relaxing his stance on Christmas, Carissa thought.

She made sure that the room was set up

for the official opening, and had a red ribbon ready to cut. The remainder of the Wylde Boys were meeting her there to sing in her father's honour, so there was a small stage at the side. Best to test the PA system, Carissa decided, and switched on the microphone.

They'd arranged to borrow two of the offices from the doctors for the backroom staff dealing with the Virtual Santa project. The team was ready in place and the phones were working, and Santa was getting changed. Quinn tested the software and the app to make sure it all worked.

Once Santa was in costume and in position, ready to talk to the kids, Quinn headed for the room where Carissa was due to make her speech to open the ward, and heard someone singing *a capella*.

Carissa.

He'd heard her sing at the carol concert, but he'd never heard her sing more than a snatch of a song entirely on her own. She'd consistently told him that she hadn't inherited her dad's talent, but he begged to differ. He loved the sound of her singing. Not wanting her to stop, he waited until she reached the end of the song before going into the room.

'Phase one's all ready to roll,' he said.

'Thanks.' She gave him a nervous smile.

He patted her arm. 'Hey. This is going to be brilliant,' he said. 'You're going to be brilliant. Go and knock everyone's socks off.'

Just as they'd arranged, Carissa took the tablet round to each child and quietly told Santa their names before she started chatting with them. The children all seemed thrilled to bits that Santa actually knew their names; even the older ones who obviously wouldn't believe in Santa any more seemed excited and couldn't quite work out how it was done.

When Carissa had spoken to the last child, Quinn patched himself through to Santa. 'Can you do me a favour, please?' he asked.

'Sure—what do you need?' Santa asked.

'Can you ask Carissa what she wants for Christmas? Don't say I asked—just keep it general.'

'Will do.' Santa paused while Quinn patched him back to Carissa.

'Hey, Carissa—Merry Carissa-mas! Ho ho ho!'

Carissa laughed. 'Very good, Santa.'

'You've heard that pun before, haven't you?' he asked wryly.

'A few times,' she said with a smile.

'You've done all this for everyone else, so

I wanted to ask you—what do you want for Christmas, young lady?'

Quinn sat up and paid attention.

Very, very close attention, as Carissa's face filled his screen. She looked wistful and longing. Did she want the same for Christmas that he did?

But then she smiled. 'I'm quite happy,' she said. 'I already have everything I could ever want, and expecting more would just be greedy.'

Arrgh. He should've known that Carissa would say something like that. It was her all over.

'But,' she said, and Quinn focused again, 'if you could see your way to sorting out peace on earth and goodwill to all men, that would be quite good.'

'I'll do my best,' Santa said.

Quinn wondered, was it true? Was Carissa saying that she didn't want anything else? Or was she too scared to ask for what she wanted because she didn't think she'd get it?

At three o'clock it was time for the official opening. Quinn slipped out of his back-seat role at that point, so he could join Carissa's family, the journalists and the visiting dignitaries for the ceremony in the main room.

'I'll keep this as short as I can,' Carissa said, 'because there's nothing worse than having to listen to someone droning on, especially when you're not feeling very well or you want to be with your sick child. But today I'm really thrilled and proud to be here. Twenty-seven years ago, I was staying in the children's ward here—I was only six weeks old, and I had a virus that meant I needed help to eat and to breathe. The staff here saved my life—not just the doctors and nurses, but the support staff who were there to help—and my dad wrote a song about it.'

At that point, the Wylde Boys quietly played the introduction to 'Santa, Bring my Baby Home for Christmas', and there was a general cheer.

'I'm honoured to say that the song found its way into people's hearts, and my mum and dad set up a trust fund from the royalties so they could give something back to the hospital that had saved their daughter. I ended up here a couple more times when I was little, and I can still remember how kind the staff were.

'So, today, I'm thrilled to be opening the new children's ward, named in honour of my parents—the Wylde Ward. It's taken a lot of time and a lot of hard work, but the team's been amazing and I'm so proud to have been a part of this. I wish my mum and dad were here to see their dream come true, but I think they're here in spirit.'

Today, Quinn knew, was the anniversary of their deaths—a day that must be so hard for her, and yet in true Carissa style she was trying to see the positive. Even though her voice had cracked on the last sentence.

'I'd like to wish all the ward's patients a very speedy recovery, and its staff all the support they'll ever need. And I'm going to shut up now because I think the best way to open the ward is with a song. Ladies and gentlemen, I give you the Wylde Ward—and the Wylde Boys!'

She cut the ribbon, and the press photographers took plenty of shots.

This time the Wylde Boys played the whole of the Santa song. Everyone in the room joined in singing the song with them at the chorus. Quinn was shocked to discover that he was singing along, too—especially when he realised that he didn't loathe the saccharine words any more. Because now he knew they were all about Carissa.

He could see the tears glistening in her eyes and he ached to hold her close, to tell her that she'd done her parents proud and she'd achieved everything she wanted. But it wasn't his place and he couldn't push in—not if it wasn't what she wanted.

The Wylde Boys played a couple more songs, including a cover of 'All I Want For Christmas is You'. Quinn caught Carissa's eye and wondered if she too remembered the moment when he'd kissed her to that song at the Winter Fantasia.

And then he saw Carissa give the very slightest nod—clearly everything had been delivered and their special guest was ready to make his appearance.

She stepped back over to the microphone. 'I believe we have a very special guest arriving to see you all.'

Santa walked in with a sled on wheels, laden with beautifully wrapped presents. And he actually had reindeer with him. Real, live reindeer. Young ones, so they were on a leading rein and not actually pulling the sled—but he could see the children's eyes grow round with pleasure as they saw the reindeer and Santa.

How Carissa had managed to get the reindeer past the health and safety people, Quinn had no idea. But right now he'd be prepared to admit that he could see the magic of Christmas. It was right there in the faces of the children.

The children were all amazed that Santa

had brought them exactly what they'd wished for. Even the seriously ill children seemed to brighten as the man in the red suit and white beard strode around, ho-ho-hoing and spending a little time to chat and laugh with each child. She'd chosen the actor to play Santa very well, Quinn thought—but then of course she had, because Carissa Wylde paid attention to all the details.

He noticed that the presents on Santa's sled weren't just for the children. Carissa had also bought gifts for all the staff on the ward, from the cleaners through to the clinical director. And Quinn would just bet she'd done the groundwork for that herself, chatting and being sweet and secretly taking notes about their dream presents. Nothing so flashy and expensive that it would embarrass the recipient but something thoughtful and tailored just to them. The junior staff looked shocked that they'd been included, and several were close to tears because they were so touched.

Carissa also gave all the back-room team a bottle of champagne and a box of seriously good chocolates each. Nobody had been left out. In fact, the only person not to have a present from Santa was Carissa herself. And Quinn could have kicked himself for not thinking about that and organising it.

The press were still taking photographs and interviewing Carissa, and even though she must be tired from all that running around and a little fed up with being forced to pose for the cameras, she didn't show it—she was gracious and sweet, and Quinn thought how much he admired her.

'That's our girl,' said Tom Wylde. His voice caught and he was clearly very emotional, as was Mary. 'Our Pete would be so proud of her.'

'She's amazing,' Quinn said softly.

Tom gave him a thoughtful look but said nothing, and Quinn knew that he needed to be careful. Until he was ready to talk to Carissa, he didn't want anyone accidentally dropping hints that he might not see himself as just her neighbour and her colleague.

Finally Santa left with his reindeer, waving and ho-ho-hoing, to cheers and applause. The Wylde Boys played a last couple of songs and then packed up their instruments. And finally Quinn finished packing up the computer equipment he'd brought in.

'He was pretty sure that Carissa would be busy with her family now, given that it was the ward opening as well as the anniversary of Pete and Isobel's deaths, but when she walked in he asked anyway. 'Do you need a lift back to Grove End Mews, or are you going some-where with your family?'

'We're all going out for a meal,' she said.

He nodded and gave her his best smile. 'Good. Have a great time.'

She rested her hand on his forearm. He could feel the warmth of her skin through his sleeve, and every nerve end felt as if it had been galvanised.

'Quinn, didn't I ask you this morning?'

'Ask me what?'

'If you'd come with us for dinner.'

'No.'

'Look, this isn't a last-minute thing. I meant to ask you. I was *sure* I already asked you and you said yes.'

Quinn knew that Carissa believed in includ-ing people. She'd been scathing about the way Tabitha's family had treated him.

She grimaced. 'Sorry. I had so many things on my list. It must've been the one thing I didn't tick off. I feel really guilty now.'

'It's fine, and anyway I'm sure your family would prefer it to be just you.'

She shook her head. 'I haven't introduced you properly yet to Granny and Gramps. Come with us, Quinn—and anyway, if it wasn't for you the virtual Santa wouldn't exist, so you're definitely part of this.'

Tom came over, clearly hearing Carissa's last words. 'You are coming with us, aren't you, Quinn? Or don't you like Asian food?'

'Actually, I do,' he said. 'Very much.'

'Good.' Tom clapped him on the back. 'Because we're going to Brick Lane, to one of the best curry houses in London.'

In the East End, too, Quinn thought, smiling; the Wyldes were proud of their heritage.

Someone had booked the restaurant, which was just as well as their party took up half the tables in the room. After a noisy few minutes everyone agreed to have a mix of dishes and share them. Somehow Quinn managed to end up being seated next to Carissa and opposite her mother's parents.

'Quinn, I didn't introduce you properly earlier,' Carissa said. 'These are my grandparents, Jennifer and William Burton.'

'Pleased to meet you,' Quinn said, shaking their hands in turn across the table.

'Granny, Gramps, this is Quinn O'Neill.'

How was she going to introduce him? he wondered. Neighbour? Colleague? Friend? Lover?

Then again, these were her grandparents, so maybe not the latter.

And they weren't lovers anyway.

Yet.

The thought made him feel hot all over. 'Quinn's my virtual Santa expert,' she explained.

'Ah, "Smart Is the New Sexy",' Jennifer said.

He groaned. 'Please tell me she didn't show you that article.'

'It was a very nice piece, sweetie,' Jennifer said, 'though it did make you sound rather mysterious.'

'Granny, if he tells you about his job, he'll—'

He waited for the 'have to kill you' joke.

But this time Carissa finished, 'End up in prison for breaking the law.'

'Right,' Jennifer said. 'And then your grandfather would have to go into court and explain that it wasn't Quinn's fault, it was a silly old woman being very silly indeed.'

There was nothing silly about Jennifer Burton, Quinn thought. He'd already noticed that everyone in Carissa's family was bright.

Despite the Burtons' posh accents being so different from the Wyldes' East London accents, the two families seemed very close. Just as she'd told him, their backgrounds made no difference. Quinn could see for himself that they really were a unit. There were no tensions, and none of the suspicion towards in-laws that Quinn's own family had demonstrated.

It was a bit hard to remember everyone else's names, though he remembered meeting George and Little George.

But the strangest thing was how he felt with the Wyldes and the Burtons. It was the first time that most of them had met him, yet he was comfortable with them and they treated him as if they'd known him for years. The complete opposite of that excruciating house party with Tabitha's family that Christmas. Here he felt accepted as part of a bigger group, and he'd never really had that before. It was a bit odd, but it was a good feeling.

'We need a toast to Pete and Isobel. We still miss you and we always will,' Tom Wylde said, lifting his glass.

Next was a toast to Carissa from William Burton. 'The best granddaughter I could ever have, and we're all so proud of you.'

And then Quinn was shocked when Carissa toasted him. 'Quinn O'Neill, who made my virtual Santa happen and wouldn't accept a single penny even though he put all the work in.'

'It wasn't rocket science. It would've been fraud to charge you anything,' Quinn protested, and everyone just laughed and clapped him on the back and drank to him anyway.

He was enjoying himself so much that he didn't realise how late it was until he glanced at his watch. He also glanced at Carissa and noticed that she looked pale and utterly exhausted.

He turned to Jennifer. 'I think I ought to drive Carissa home. She's been up since the crack of dawn, and she's been working crazy hours to get everything sorted for today.'

'Good idea,' Jennifer said. 'The poor lamb looks as if she's about to crash. She said you live very near her.'

'Three doors down,' Quinn said. 'I'll take care of her.'

Jennifer held his gaze for a moment, and it felt as if she was looking into his soul. Judging him. Checking that he really would take care of Carissa. And then she smiled. 'Good.'

So he had Carissa's grandmother's approval, at least. That was a start.

It took a while to say goodbye to everyone, but finally Quinn drove Carissa back across London to Grove End Mews.

'It was a really good day,' he said. 'I bet your parents are looking down, as proud as anything. You were brilliant.'

'It was teamwork,' she said. 'It wouldn't have happened without my team.'

'But the team couldn't have done it without you organising it.' He parked outside his house. 'Come and sit down for a few minutes. I'll make you a hot drink.'

She followed him into his house, took off her jacket and shoes and curled up on his sofa.

'Hot milk?' he asked.

She smiled at him, so sweetly that it made his heart ache. 'That'd be lovely, thanks.'

He poured milk into a mug and put it into the microwave for a couple of minutes to heat through. But by the time he walked back into the living room Carissa had fallen asleep on the sofa.

She looked so cute.

It was a shame to wake her, but Quinn knew he had to. He stroked her cheek. 'Carissa?'

'Mmm,' she said, and snuggled into the cushions.

Waking her up and making her go out into the cold would be mean, he decided—and he'd changed his sheets that morning anyway. So, instead of waking her, he took her glasses off and put them safely on the mantelpiece, then picked her up.

Funny, when he'd thought of carrying her to his bed, it hadn't been like this. In his mind she'd been wide awake and kissing him all the way.

But right now she was just snuggled against him, her arms wrapped round his neck, all warm and sweet and soft. And what he felt most was protective of her.

He pushed the duvet to one side and gently laid her on the mattress.

Should he undress her? No, that felt a bit sleazy. He just about resisted the temptation to climb in beside her and hold her close, and instead tucked her in.

She shifted onto her side; he watched her for a moment, amused that she slept like the dead. Then again, it had been a long and emotional day for her. Right now she really needed some sleep.

'Sweet dreams, Carissa,' he whispered, then quietly took a spare blanket and pillow from the shelf in his wardrobe and took them through to the living room. Then he made himself comfortable on the sofa. Tomorrow, he thought, maybe they'd talk. And their 'magic of Christmas' dates could maybe change from being a wager to being real.

CHAPTER ELEVEN

CARISSA WOKE, WARM and comfortable…and yet the light felt wrong. Trying to work out why, she shifted position and opened her eyes—and realised immediately that this wasn't her bedroom. And it most definitely wasn't her bed.

The room was stark, functional and very masculine: it had to be Quinn's bedroom, because she couldn't remember a thing after curling up on his sofa last night while he'd gone into the kitchen to make her some hot milk.

But did this mean that Quinn had carried her to his bed?

Had he shared the bed with her?

Embarrassed and feeling hot all over, she sat up. There was no dent in the pillow next to hers, but then again if he had a latex or memory foam pillow there wouldn't be a dent. She slid her hand across the sheet on the other side of the bed; it was stone cold, so if he *had* slept with her he'd got up quite a long time ago.

And she was fully clothed—which meant he'd been careful with her privacy and her dignity. Though she had no idea how she'd got here. Had he carried her? Because that was totally undignified. And if she'd been snoring or drooling…

She glanced at her watch. Oh, help. It was already half past seven. No way would she be at her desk by eight-thirty.

She slid out of bed and went in search of Quinn. The first thing she needed to do was apologise. And then she needed to find out what had happened.

He wasn't in the living room or his kitchen. Feeling as if she was prying, she went down the corridor and rapped on the open door at the end.

'Yes?'

She leaned round the door. Quinn was working at his desk—looking totally edible in another of his faded T-shirts and a little too much stubble.

'I—um— Good morning.'

He smiled at her, and she went weak at the knees. Not good.

'Morning,' he said. 'Did you sleep well?'

'I… Yes.' And she needed to deal with the big issue right now. 'Quinn, I'm so sorry about last night. I don't remember a thing.'

His eyes crinkled at the corners, but she knew he was laughing with her rather than at her. 'It's fine. Nothing to worry about at all. You'd had a long day, and after all that adrenalin it was obvious you were going to crash out and sleep like the dead.'

'But I put you out.'

'It's fine. I just carried you into my room so you'd be more comfortable. And it was laundry day yesterday, so the sheets were clean.'

She felt her face heat. 'Thank you. But I would've been fine if you'd just woken me up and sent me home.'

His smile broadened. 'I don't think a hurricane could've woken you last night. And you didn't put me out. My sofa's comfortable enough.'

So he hadn't shared the bed with her. She wasn't sure whether to be relieved or disappointed. But she was grateful that he'd cleared it up without embarrassing her. 'Thank you.'

'Any time.' He saved his file and stood up. 'I could do with some coffee. Stay and have some breakfast with me?'

This was her excuse to leave—but then again, if she was going to be late for work anyway, she might as well take another few minutes now and have breakfast with him. It would at least give her another chance to apologise.

'Yes, I'd like that. Thank you.'

'Come through.'

He wouldn't let her help make breakfast, which made her feel a bit like a spoiled brat; but his coffee was good and went a long way to restoring her.

'Is a bacon sandwich OK with you?'

'Very OK, thank you,' she said.

And within a minute of him putting bacon under the grill, her mouth was watering at the scent.

'I'm afraid you have to slum it a bit today,' he said. 'I guess normally you'd have kedgeree or devilled kidneys, all served on silver platters with domed lids.'

She knew he was teasing her, and pulled a face. 'I hate kidneys and kedgeree. Though I do like smoked salmon and scrambled eggs. And,' she confessed, 'Granny and Gramps do have silver flatware with domed lids.'

'Well, I have much less washing-up,' he said with a grin.

'You could have made porridge,' she said.

He rolled his eyes. 'Because it's healthy?'

She indicated her hair, and he laughed, clearly following her train of thought. 'Ah, right. And the test would be whether I got it too hot, too cold or just right.' He paused. 'Or was it salt and sweet?'

'For the record, I like my porridge with fresh blueberries, a teaspoon of flaxseed, a teaspoon of pumpkin seeds and a sprinkle of cinnamon,' she said.

'You *would*.' He buttered some bread. 'So, Goldilocks, was the bed too hard or too soft?'

'Just right.' Or it would have been had Quinn been in it with her. But he'd been a perfect gentleman. Or did that mean he wasn't interested and she was about to make a fool of herself? Right now, he was incredibly hard to read. And she took refuge in silence, not wanting to get things wrong.

'Glad to hear it,' he said lightly. He finished making her sandwich and handed it to her on a plate. 'Help yourself to ketchup.'

'Thanks.' She ate a bite as he finished making his own sandwich and sat opposite her. 'This is fabulous.'

'Pleasure.'

Carissa had eaten with Quinn a few times now, but breakfast this morning seemed somehow much more intimate. Especially as she'd spent last night sleeping in his bed—despite the fact that he'd slept on his sofa.

She felt oddly shy with him and didn't have a clue what to say. Finally, she glanced at her watch. 'I really have to be going. Thanks for last night. And breakfast.' Taking a risk, she pushed her chair back, walked over to him and hugged him. 'Thanks for everything.'

Quinn knew that this was the moment when he should ask Carissa if he could see her again. But without the virtual Santa, the proof of Christmas magic and the surveillance stuff at the refuge, he had no reason to see her other than as a neighbour. Suggesting more would mean making this thing between them real. They'd be dating officially.

Panic seeped through him. What if he asked her, and she said no?

Or, even more scarily, what if she said yes?

Then the moment passed.

'I'm going to be late for the office this morning,' Carissa said. 'I need a shower and to change. Just as well I wear my hair back at work or it'd be a right mess. I, um, I'd better go. Thanks again for everything.'

'Pleasure.' He went downstairs with her to the front door. 'See you around.'

'Yeah.'

When the door closed behind her, Quinn could have kicked himself for not arranging to see her again. Preferably tonight. But he couldn't think of a way to ask her now.

And Carissa had been all bright and breezy as she'd left. Had that been bravado, or was it the way she really felt? He had no idea. And asking her was out of the question.

He went back to the kitchen, washed up and left the dishes to drain while he cleared everything away, then headed for his desk. At least he had new toys to play with, or rather develop. He spent the day trying to play it cool, and tried not to be to disappointed when she didn't call or text him.

He lasted one more day before he called her.

'Hey—how's it going?' he asked.

'Fine. You?'

'Yes.' He paused. 'Are you busy at work?'

'Pretty much,' she said. 'And you?'

'Uh-huh.' Oh, for pity's sake, why was he pussyfooting around? Why was he being so inarticulate? Why didn't he just ask her out? It didn't matter where they went. It was being with her that mattered most.

He was just about to open his mouth and suggest they went skating again when she said, 'Quinn, it's Christmas in a couple of days.'

'Ye-es.'

'I know you hate the day, so I'm guessing you haven't arranged anything better than heated-up pizza.'

'A toasted sandwich, actually,' he said, and she laughed.

'I can offer you something a bit better than that. Come and have Christmas dinner with me.'

Did she mean just the two of them?

'Aren't you joining your family?' he asked.

'No. I'm going to Nan and Poppy's for Boxing Day. Granny and Gramps will be there too.'

It seemed a bit odd that a woman who loved Christmas as much as Carissa did would spend the day on her own. Or maybe she did a stint in a soup kitchen or something. That would be just like her. Quiet, practical, and sorting things out without making a big fuss about it.

'What time do you want me to come over?' he asked.

'About two?' she suggested.

It definitely sounded as if she was doing a soup-kitchen stint first. 'Anything I can do or bring?'

'No, and just yourself,' she said.

Neither of them had spoken about exchanging presents. But he could hardly go to Christmas dinner at her place empty-handed.

What did you buy a woman who had pretty much everything?

He rang the local florist and sweet-talked

them into doing him a hand-tied bouquet for Christmas Eve. A bottle of champagne and a box of good chocolates would work, too. And he just hoped that Carissa would like them all.

Christmas Day.

It was the first time Quinn had looked forward to it ever since he could remember.

He'd sent the obligatory formal cards to his aunt, uncle and cousins and received equally stiff and formal greetings in return. Not that he'd bothered putting his cards up on the mantelpiece. It was way too much clutter for his liking. Just as he hadn't bothered with a tree or any kind of Christmas decorations.

Bah, humbug.

At two o'clock he walked round to Carissa's house and rang the bell.

She answered the door, wearing a crimson velvet dress. She looked absolutely stunning. He wanted to kiss her—really kiss her—but maybe this wasn't the place. In her doorway, in front of the whole mews, was maybe a little too public.

He handed her the flowers and her smile made his heart skip a beat.

'Oh, Quinn, they're gorgeous! Thank you. It wasn't necessary, but they're very much appreciated.'

'And my contribution to dinner.' He gave her the champagne and the chocolates.

She kissed him on the cheek, and his skin tingled.

'How lovely. Thank you, Quinn. Come up.'

He had been expecting it to be just the two of them, but then she shepherded him into the dining room. The table was set with a white damask tablecloth, polished silver cutlery and orange-and-spice scented candles. Several elderly people were already sitting there, chatting to each to each other. There was a place at the head of the table that was clearly reserved for Carissa and an empty place at the other end that he assumed was going to be his. Everyone's faces were a little familiar, though he couldn't quite place them.

Carissa introduced him to everyone and then he realised: they were all from Grove End Mews. She'd clearly invited the people who didn't have family nearby and would be spending Christmas Day on their own if she hadn't offered them somewhere to go. Given her fairy-godmother habit, he wasn't too surprised. And he couldn't be mean-spirited enough to be disappointed that it wasn't going to be the quiet, romantic Christmas he'd been fantasising about.

'Can I help with anything?' he asked.

'You can take the serving dishes in, if you like,' she said. 'And can you carve?'

'Not brilliantly,' he admitted. On the rare occasions that he entertained, it was usually in a restaurant.

'OK. I'll handle that bit.'

He took in the dishes of vegetables and trimmings, and then the platter containing an enormous turkey, which he set in front of Carissa's seat. Then he opened the champagne and poured a glass for everyone while she carved.

Being Carissa, she insisted that everyone pull Christmas crackers, share the terrible jokes and wear party hats at the table. But the gifts weren't like the usual contents of crackers, tape measures and thimbles and pens that stopped working within half a sentence: she'd swapped them for little boxes of very nice truffles.

Quinn had expected to be on the edges of the conversation, but was pleasantly surprised at being included. And hearing septuagenarians' stories of Christmases past turned out to be fascinating.

After lunch, there were several rounds of board games and card games where Quinn felt a little more out of place, so he slipped out quietly to the kitchen and dealt with the washing-up.

Carissa walked in and caught him. 'You really shouldn't have,' she scolded, 'but thank you.'

Everyone was too full to eat anything more than a small slice of Christmas cake in the early evening. Quinn saw some of the more elderly guests back safely to their own homes, as it was frosty and slippery outside. And then he was back in his own house.

Alone.

The way he'd always used to like it, but now it felt like an anti-climax. And his house felt so stark and impersonal after the warmth of Carissa's house. Funny how she'd changed his life so much in a few short weeks.

His phone beeped.

He glanced at the screen and saw there was a text from her.

Come and have a glass of champagne with me.

This time, he knew, it would be just the two of them.

CHAPTER TWELVE

WHEN CARISSA OPENED her front door and smiled, Quinn's knees went weak. While he'd been seeing their neighbours safely back to their own homes, she'd loosened her hair; now it flowed over her shoulders like spun silk. And that dress was a knockout. She looked like all his dreams rolled into one.

'Come in,' she said.

'It's just you and me?' he checked.

She nodded. 'Just you and me.' She looked suddenly nervous. 'Is that OK?'

'More than OK,' he said softly.

'Sorry, I should've told you earlier that I normally do Christmas here in the mews. I cook a Christmas dinner for those who won't really get one otherwise.'

He smiled. 'Being a fairy godmother.' Her favourite thing, he'd come to realise.

'I just like making people happy.' Her eyes

were wide and entreating. 'Is that such a bad thing?'

'No,' he admitted. 'And I enjoyed today.'

'Really?' She looked uncertain, vulnerable, and he wanted to hug her and tell her that everything was just fine.

'Really,' he said. 'I'm not just being polite. I had a good time.'

'I'm glad,' she said. 'Come up.'

In her living room, she poured two glasses of champagne and handed one to him. 'Merry Christmas,' she said.

'Merry Christmas,' he echoed, lifting his glass. 'And here's to you.'

'Me?' She sounded surprised. 'Why?'

'Because you're what's made Christmas special for me. It's the first time I've enjoyed the day in years and years.' Maybe the first time ever, though he didn't want to make her feel bad by telling her that.

'Even though I had a house full of people?'

'That's what makes you *you*,' he said, and smiled. He took a sip of champagne. 'I guess the skating rink won't be open tonight, or if it is it'll have been booked up for months. Otherwise I'd take you there tonight.'

'How about a second-best alternative to skating?' she asked.

'What do you have in mind?'

'Dance with me?'

Which meant she'd be in his arms. Perfect. 'I'd love to.'

Unlike Quinn, Carissa kept her music in hard copy. He'd noticed that she'd been playing a mix of seasonal pop songs and Christmas carols all day, and assumed it would be more of the same. When she put on a CD, Quinn recognised the tune as soon as the first few bars floated into the air. The song he'd kissed her to at the Winter Fantasia.

'All I Want for Christmas is You.'

'I remember them playing that at the Winter Fantasia,' she said quietly.

So she was thinking of that night, too? He looked her straight in the eye. She was so soft, so sweet—and he wanted her more than he'd wanted anything in his life. 'Me, too. And that's a very appropriate song choice,' he said, equally quietly.

Her pupils were huge, as if she was remembering the way he'd kissed her that night. The way he wanted to kiss her right now. 'Carissa,' he said, and drew her into his arms. He wished she'd chosen something smoochy. This song was slightly too fast to sway to, really.

'I can't stop thinking about you,' she confessed.

That made it was easy for him to admit it, too. 'I can't stop thinking about you either.'

'So what are we going to do about this?' she asked.

'I know what I want to do right now,' he said, and stroked her face. 'I want to kiss you again. The way I kissed you that night.'

'Yes,' she breathed.

He dipped his head and brushed his mouth lightly against hers, and every nerve end in his lips tingled. It was good, but not enough. Never enough. He caught her lower lip between his, nipped gently, and she opened her mouth to let him deepen the kiss.

Time seemed to stand still. He could stay here, kissing her, for ever, with his arms wrapped tightly round her waist and her arms wrapped round his neck. He loved the way her body felt against his, pliant and curvy and utterly delectable.

All the lights on the Christmas tree were twinkling, and the scent of clean, sharp pine mingled with the soft floral scent she wore.

He drew back slightly so he could look her straight in the eye and whispered, 'You were right about the magic of Christmas, Carissa. It exists all right. And it's you—it's all you. The way you make me feel amazes me. I never thought I could feel like this.' He shook his head in wonder. 'When you smile at me, it's as if the whole room's lit up with starbursts.'

It was how she felt, too; there was a kind of sparkle in the air and, for her, it came from him.

She laid her palm against his face. Although he'd shaved that morning, now there was the faintest hint of stubble against her skin, and it made a shiver of desire skitter all the way down her spine. 'Quinn.'

'I should go home right now,' he said.

But she could see in his face that he didn't want to go. He was trying to be honourable and do the right thing by her.

Maybe she didn't want him to do the right thing.

Maybe she wanted him to do exactly what she thought he wanted to do. Hoped he wanted to do. 'Or else?' she tested.

He was actually shaking now. 'The other night,' he said, 'when I carried you to my bed, you were warm and soft and sweet. And I very nearly climbed into bed beside you. I wanted to hold you close, pillow your head on my shoulder, and wake up with you in my arms.' He stole a kiss. 'But then again you were spark out. It wouldn't have been fair to you. But, just so you know, it tore me apart to leave you.'

Quinn O'Neill was a man with a good heart.

An honourable man. A man, Carissa thought, that she could trust. And this time it wouldn't all go pear-shaped. He wasn't angry and self-centred, like Justin. And he would never, ever hurt her.

'Besides,' he added, 'what I really wanted to do was carry you to my bed while you were wide awake and kissing me, wanting me every bit as much as I want you.'

That was what she wanted, too.

'We're in my house,' she pointed out.

'Three doors down. Which isn't that much further to carry you.'

The thought made her weak at the knees.

But she didn't want him to know quite how much he affected her. 'Caveman,' she teased.

'Goes with the Y chromosome,' he shot back.

'Maybe,' she said, 'I'd rather you conserved your strength.'

'Ah. So all she wants is the use of my biceps to haul another Christmas tree around.'

'Not necessarily,' she said.

'So what do you have in mind?'

Something very, very delicious. Something she thought he might want just as much as she wanted. 'What exactly,' she asked, 'would be the difference between carrying me to your bed and carrying me to mine?'

'For a start, I know where my bedroom is.'

'Did you know there's such a thing as directions?' Sparring with him like this was fun. And it took the edge off the sudden fear and worry that this would all go wrong, the way it had with Justin.

'Directions? Hmm. So there are.'

He kissed her slowly, thoroughly, and when he lifted his head again his mouth was swollen and reddened. She'd just bet hers was in a similar state.

'Supposing I do this?' he asked, and lifted her up. 'Now—these directions you were talking about?'

She slid her arms round his neck. 'Out of the door, up the stairs, first left. Or maybe you'd prefer me to walk up the stairs.'

'No chance. You're not heavy.'

'And you have good biceps,' she teased. 'For carrying Christmas trees.'

'And for carrying you,' he said, and proceeded to carry her out of her living room and up the stairs. He paused outside her room. 'Here?'

'Here,' she confirmed.

He set her back on her feet but he made sure that her whole body was plastered against his on the way down. And it sent a thrill all the way through her.

'I love that dress,' he said huskily, 'but right now I really want to take it off you. Unwrap you.'

Like a Christmas present, she thought—except it was a mutual one and she wanted to do exactly the same to him. 'Sounds good to me.'

'So can I?'

In answer, she sashayed into the room and switched on her bedside light. She was glad she'd closed the curtains earlier. She paused long enough to light the scented candle she kept on top of her bedside cabinet, then turned the bedside light off.

The light was gentle and kind: bright enough for her to see him but dim enough for her not to feel exposed and raw.

He followed her in to the room. 'Turn round,' he said.

She did so, and he unzipped her dress to her waist. Very, very slowly.

Gently, he moved her hair over her shoulder and then pushed the crimson velvet over her shoulders, baring her back.

'You're so beautiful,' he said. 'It makes me want to do this.'

She felt him kiss his way down her spine, and shivered. She wanted this, too. So very much.

He undid the zip the rest of the way and let

her dress fall to the floor. Then he pushed the shoulder straps of her bra out of the way and kissed her bare shoulders. She loved the feel of his lips against her skin, warm and gentle and coaxing.

Then he turned her to face him.

'You're beautiful,' he said. 'Your skin's so soft and you smell so good.'

She stroked his face with a shaking hand. 'And you're fully clothed still.'

'I'm in your hands,' he said. 'Do what you will with me.'

It was an offer she would enjoy accepting.

He wore a plain cream shirt with a button-down collar. The copper-coloured buttons glinted in the candlelight and she undid them one by one, stroking each centimetre of skin that she uncovered.

'Smart is *definitely* the new sexy,' she breathed, when she'd finally finished taking off his shirt.

He gave her a half-smile that made her pulse speed up a notch. 'Thank you.'

She spread her hands across his pectoral muscles. 'You're beautiful, Quinn. And you feel as good as you look.' And she couldn't ever remember wanting anyone so much.

He took her hand, brought it up to his mouth, kissed her palm and folded his fingers over the kiss. Carissa's knees went weak again. How did he affect her like this?

Then he unsnapped her bra; she felt shy now, but he wouldn't let her cover herself with her hands. Instead, he caught them and drew them to his mouth, this time kissing each knuckle in turn. 'Don't be afraid. I'm not going to hurt you.'

She knew that, and let her hands fall to her sides. 'Condom,' she whispered. 'Do you have one?'

Shock skittered across his face; clearly he hadn't been planning this either. 'Give me a second,' he said, took his wallet from his pocket and opened it.

She thought, If he doesn't have a condom, then we have to stop right now. On Christmas night, nowhere would be open to sell condoms. Embarrassment and shame flooded through her.

But then he exhaled sharply. 'Yes, I do.'

At least she knew now that he hadn't come here expecting to sleep with her; he'd come to drink champagne with her, to spend time with her. But the spiralling need for each other had taken them both by surprise.

'OK,' she said, feeling much more confident. 'Now lose the trousers.'

'You want me to strip for you?'

'It's Christmas. Humour me.'

He laughed, and stripped very, very slowly.

And now they were both down to their underwear.

He stripped off his socks, and gestured to her.

She stripped off her tights.

And then she would have felt shy, except Quinn took her hand and drew her gently to him, then kissed her until her knees had turned to mush and her head was going the same way.

And then he pushed her duvet aside, lifted her up, and settled her back against the pillows, and she stopped thinking altogether.

Quinn woke the next morning feeling warm and comfortable. He was flat on his back; there was a head on his shoulder and an arm round his waist.

Carissa.

He thought about the way they'd made love last night, the way she'd given herself to him. The connection had been like nothing he'd ever known.

It was still relatively early. He considered waking her with a kiss and making love with her again; but then he remembered that it was Boxing Day, and he knew she was planning to spend the day with her family.

Would she ask him to go with her, the way she'd asked him to join them all for dinner after the opening of the Wylde Ward? Though this time she'd be introducing him to everyone as her partner rather than her colleague.

He wasn't sure he was ready for that.

He'd liked the members of her family he'd met admittedly, and he'd got on well enough with them—but that had been when they'd seen him as her colleague and her neighbour. Their reactions to him might be very different when they knew he was more than that.

He wasn't good at closeness. And he didn't want to hurt her or to make her feel he was rejecting her or her family when he finally had to let her go, as he inevitably would. How was he going to fix this?

Normally, when he needed to think about something, he went for a run. Maybe that was what he needed right now: a run through Grove End Park, so the wintry morning air would bring back his common sense and give him a sense of perspective.

He didn't want to wake Carissa and explain—right now he didn't have the words to do it—but once he'd got his head in the right place again maybe they could talk.

Gently, he moved her hand away from his waist and slid out of the bed. He'd just grabbed his clothes and was intending to tiptoe out to the landing to get dressed without waking her when he heard Carissa ask quietly, 'Quinn? Where are you going?'

Too late.

She was already awake.

And she'd caught him in the middle of sneaking out.

'I—um…' He still didn't have the right words to explain; he couldn't even really explain it to himself. But it was a sick, sliding feeling of panic and he couldn't stop it.

'Were you going to leave without telling me?'

Put like that, it sounded bad. Not just sounded—it *was* bad. He turned to her face her. 'I'm sorry.'

She sat up, holding the duvet round herself, looking hurt. 'I thought, after last night…'

Yeah. So had he. He raked a hand through his hair. 'It's complicated.'

'Try me.'

'I want this to be different. But…' He shook his head. 'I'm just not good at this stuff, Carissa. I've never been good at being close to people. The only time I really, really tried, I got it so badly wrong it's untrue.'

She went white. 'Are you still in love with Tabitha?'

'No. I stopped loving her a long time ago. Though I admit I haven't made much effort to get close to anyone since her.' Apart from Carissa. And he'd made a mess of that, too. He sighed. 'I'm not good at family stuff either.'

'What makes you say that? I mean, I know Tabitha's family wasn't very nice to you, but that was their problem, not yours.'

'I don't normally talk about it.'

'Well, there's a surprise,' she drawled.

Ouch. He knew he deserved that. And he also knew that she deserved the truth.

'Let me just get dressed,' he said, and pulled his clothes on before sitting on the edge of her bed. Not close enough to touch her—if he was going to tell her everything, then he couldn't handle the extra distraction.

And then, finally, he began to talk.

'I was brought up by my aunt and uncle.' He looked away. 'My mum didn't want me—I was in the way of her following her dreams. When I was six months old my aunt and uncle were supposed to look after me just for the weekend, to give her a break.

'But then she called them and said she wasn't coming back. She said she was about to get on a plane to America, and she knew they'd be able to give me a better life than she could, so she was leaving me with them to be brought up. And then she hung up and caught her plane, and I never saw her again.'

Carissa frowned. 'What about your dad? Didn't he come and get you? Or did he go to America with her?'

'Nobody actually knew who my dad was,' Quinn said. 'So I couldn't really answer your question that time about whether I come from a line of scientists and inventors. Because I really don't have a clue who he was, and my mother would never say.'

She bit her lip. 'I'm sorry.'

He shrugged. 'It's not your fault.'

'Quinn, I really don't understand what's going on here. I don't understand why you wanted to go without even saying goodbye.'

That was an easy one to answer. 'Because you need to be with your family, and I'm going to be in the way.'

'But they liked you. You'd be welcome to join us today. More than welcome.'

He shook his head. 'I can't.'

'Why not? They're not like Tabitha's family. They wouldn't be mean. I mean, you met them, Quinn. You came out for dinner with us. You know they're nice.' Hurt widened her eyes.

'I'm not good at family stuff,' he said again. 'When I grew up, I always knew I was in the way. My aunt and uncle had a corner shop and three boys as it was—they didn't need an extra child to clothe and feed. I was a burden.'

'But they still brought you up.'

In typical Carissa fashion, she was trying to find the bright side. Except there wasn't one. He'd just been lonely and miserable. 'Yes.' He smiled thinly. 'Though I was always conscious that they'd been charitable.'

'Maybe they were just really angry with your mum for letting you down,' she suggested, 'and you were too young to realise that and you thought they were angry with you, when actually they weren't.'

He'd never thought of that before.

But he wasn't so sure that was the truth either. 'I didn't fit in,' Quinn said, 'and it always seemed worse at Christmas. A time when families are all meant to be close and loving, and mine just seemed to be full of arguments about money and who was supposed to be doing what in the shop. Obviously my mum didn't ever send anything to help pay for my food, clothes or school trips.' He shrugged. 'I did try contacting her a couple of times, but she made it clear that she didn't want to know. She'd found herself a new life, one that didn't have room for me.'

'I'm sorry. That's rough on you,' she said.

He shook his head. 'Don't pity me. I think

she was right—I was better off without her, because she wouldn't have been good for me.'

'What about your aunt and uncle?' she asked.

'I just never really felt part of the family.'

'Maybe they were just not very good at emotional stuff and talking about their feelings,' Carissa said.

Which was the point. He wasn't either. How could he make her understand how out on a limb he'd always felt?

'I found out I was really good at maths and physics at school. I took my exams early and I was planning a career in computer programming. My aunt and uncle wanted me to leave school at sixteen and work in the shop with my cousins, but I wanted to stay on to do my A levels and maybe go to university.'

Again, he looked away. 'They wouldn't hear of it. My cousins had all left school at sixteen and gone into the family business. Nobody in our family went to university. Ever.' He'd never talked about this before. But maybe, just maybe, if he told her, she'd understand. 'They said I had to leave school and work in the shop because I owed them for taking me in.'

She blew out a breath. 'That's pretty harsh. But maybe they were panicking, Quinn. You were about to do something nobody else in your family had ever done, and they didn't have a clue how to support you through it.'

He shrugged. 'Anyway, I left and learned to support myself.'

Her eyes widened. 'You left home and supported yourself at sixteen?'

He shrugged again. 'It was the only way I could do it. I had a weekend job that paid the rent on my bedsit and my food, and I went to school to study for my A levels during the week.'

'Being independent so young... I couldn't have done it. You're pretty amazing for getting through that,' she said. 'But your uncle and aunt are proud of you now, surely?'

'It's com—' he began.

'—plicated,' she finished, and shook her head. 'Quinn, it could be simple, if you let it.'

'How?'

'I'll tell you what I see,' she said. 'I see a man who was let down by his mum and always thought he wasn't good enough because she didn't want him, so he never really let himself get close to anyone. He worked and worked and worked to get where he is now. He made a few mistakes along the way—as anyone would, because he's only human. He picked the wrong person to fall in love with, someone who made him feel that he still wasn't good enough, despite how much he'd achieved.

'And now he believes what other people made him think about himself. He thinks he isn't good enough and he won't give himself a chance. But all he has to do is look at himself and see who he really is. Believe in himself.'

Quinn didn't have any answers to that.

She looked thoughtful. 'You once told me if you realised you'd picked the wrong person, you could just walk away.'

Ice trickled down his spine. What exactly was she saying?

'But sometimes,' she said softly, 'you have to walk away even if you think it's the right person.'

He might be inadequate, but he wasn't a coward. He met her head on. 'Are you saying you're going to walk away from me?'

She bit her lip. 'This isn't going to work, Quinn. Not until you can see yourself and accept yourself for who you really are. If you can't do that, you'll never be able to really accept that someone can love you, and you won't be able to let yourself go enough to really love them back. And that isn't fair on anyone.'

He had no words. None at all. Any articulation he'd ever had simply deserted him. All he could do was stare at her.

She was breaking up with him.

'Go home, Quinn,' she said.

Yup. She was definitely breaking up with him. Asking him to leave.

There wasn't any point in trying to change her mind. He knew he wasn't enough for her. Just as he hadn't been enough, all the way through his life. Nothing had changed. So he simply got up, walked out of the room and walked out of her life.

Every nerve in Carissa's body screamed to her to call him back. To run after him, regardless of the fact that she wasn't wearing a stitch of clothing. He was so lost, so lonely—and throwing him out was cruel.

Then again, she knew she was doing the right thing. Being cruel to be kind. Because at the end of the day Quinn O'Neill was the only person who could make Quinn O'Neill see himself for who he really was. She could talk and talk and tell him until she was blue in the face, but until he was ready to believe her he simply wouldn't listen and she would be wasting her breath.

She just hoped that he could do it.

And that then he'd be ready to come back and meet her halfway.

She stayed exactly where she was for

the next half an hour, sitting with her arms wrapped round her legs and her chin resting on her knees, forcing herself not to cry. She'd done the right thing for both of them. And she knew it. She just wished it didn't feel as if her heart had been ripped out and hung up to dry.

Washing her hair and having a shower didn't make her feel any better.

She put on her make-up and stared at her reflection in the mirror. 'Right, Carissa Wylde— you're going to Nan and Poppy's, you're going to pretend that last night never happened, and you're going to smile your face off because it's Christmas and everyone knows you really love Christmas,' she told herself out loud. If she wasn't smiling, her family would notice and they'd guess why. She didn't want to make them worry about her and she most definitely didn't want to discuss what had gone wrong with Quinn,

Inside, her heart was in shreds. But she wasn't going to let anyone see.

'Bring it on. I love Christmas,' she said, and went out to her car.

CHAPTER THIRTEEN

ON HER DAYS away from the office, Carissa would normally have enjoying plotting things for Project Sparkle—but right now she found herself going through the motions. Quinn hadn't come back. He hadn't texted her, or called, or emailed. And, much as she missed him and she was desperate to know how he was, she also knew that if they were to stand any kind of chance of coming through this, she had to keep her distance until he was ready.

If only it wasn't so hard.

And what if he didn't come back?

The thought was so scary that she actually stopped breathing for a moment. But then she shook herself. She'd survive. Of course she would. She'd got over what had happened with Justin. But it would take her a long, long time to get over Quinn.

'What do you want, Mara?' Quinn asked when he answered the video call.

'You look terrible,' she said.

'Well, hello to you, too. Don't pull your punches, will you?' he said wryly.

'Quinn, you've worked every day since Christmas. Normal people take time off to spend with their families.'

'There's no need. I don't have a family to spend it with,' he pointed out. It wasn't strictly true, but he'd spent enough time with his family begrudging him. He was better off on his own.

'What about Carissa?' Mara asked.

'What about Carissa?' he fenced.

'All the charity work you started doing— you normally just donate a huge sum of money if someone asks you for help, something big enough so people won't push you to get involved and give personal time and effort. This time you did actually get involved—and it's because of her.'

He didn't answer.

'Quinn, don't be difficult. Whatever's happened between you, why don't you just talk to her and sort it out?'

'What makes you think there's a problem?' he asked.

'Because you're a guy and you believe in being strong and silent,' Mara said. 'Look, if you've been an idiot, just buy her some chocolates or flowers, apologise, grovel a bit and sort it out.'

'And if she's the one who dumped me?' Quinn tested.

'Apart from the fact that in all the years I've known you, women have queued up to date you and try to get you to commit, and you're always the one who does the dumping,' Mara said, 'there's the way Carissa was looking at you when we went to the safe house. She likes you. More than likes you. And you obviously like her, because you dated her for longer than anyone *ever.*'

'We weren't dating,' Quinn protested. 'It was a bet.'

'Yeah, right,' Mara said scornfully. 'Pull the other one—it's got bells on. Quinn, when you were with her you looked happier than I've ever known you. You're being an idiot. Talk to her.'

Right at that point, he couldn't.

But little bits of their last conversation kept flicking into his head at odd times, even when he was trying to concentrate on his work. Things that made him think about his family. Family was important to Carissa, yet he'd turned his back on his.

Maybe they were just really angry with your mum for letting you down...

Maybe they were just not very good at emotional stuff and talking about their feelings...

Maybe they were panicking...they didn't have a clue how to support you...

Was she right?

There was only one way to find out.

He picked up the phone. It had been years since he'd spoken to his cousins. He'd never really been close to then. The oldest, Sam, was ten years older than he was, and as a teenager hadn't been interested in spending time with a small child. Max was five years older, and they'd had nothing in common. Tim, the youngest, was the same age—but Tim had always been into football and had mocked Quinn for being a bookish nerd.

Sam, as the oldest, had the most life experience, so he was likely to be the most approachable. Quinn hoped.

He dialled his number, hoping that Sam would actually be there. To his relief, Sam answered. 'Sam? It's Quinn.'

'Quinn?' Sam sounded surprised. 'What do you want?'

Not the best of openings but, then again, how long had it been since they'd talked? 'Just ringing to wish you a happy new year.' Not the whole truth, but it was a start.

'Uh-huh.' Sam coughed. 'Don't take this the

wrong way—but you never call to wish us a happy new year.'

'Maybe I'm trying to turn over a new leaf.' Quinn sighed. 'OK. I know it's a lot to ask, and a lot of things have gone wrong in the past, but it's about time they were sorted out. I wondered if we could talk?'

'Well—I guess. When and where?'

Didn't they always say there was no time like the present? 'Today?'

'Where are you?'

'London. I can be with you in a couple of hours.'

Sam paused, and for a moment Quinn thought he was going to say no. 'OK. I'll get cover for my shift. Do Mum and Dad know you're coming?'

'No. And I thought we could meet on neutral ground so there's no pressure on anyone.'

'Just you and me, then. OK. Do you know the café on Borough Street? There's parking on the road outside.'

'OK. See you there.'

Quinn felt ridiculously nervous as he drove to Birmingham. He couldn't fix the past, but maybe he could put it to rest and start to look to the future. Make things different.

Sam was already in the café when he walked in, and stood up to shake Quinn's hand. 'Good to see you.' He scrutinised Quinn closely. 'Whatever you're doing now, it suits you.'

'Same old nerdy stuff,' Quinn said wryly. And then, surprising himself, he blurted out, 'I met someone.'

'I wondered,' Sam said. 'Because it changes you when you meet someone.'

The warmth in Sam's expression told Quinn that he'd made the right decision. His cousin understood. And there was a chance that they could start to fix things 'Yeah.'

'Let me get us a coffee,' Sam said, and caught the waitress's eye.

Once they'd ordered, he said, 'So that's what this is really about?'

'Yes and no,' Quinn said. 'She's made me see that maybe I got it wrong about the past.'

'Walking out on us, you mean? That really hurt Mum and Dad.'

'I know. And I'm sorry for that. I didn't do it to hurt them.' Quinn sighed. 'I just knew I didn't want the life they planned for me, and I couldn't see any other way out.'

'And you were so different from us. None of us really understood you, and I guess Mum and Dad found it hard to get through to you,' Sam said. 'Now I'm a dad, I see things differently. You want your kids to have the best, and they don't always want the same things for themselves that you want for them. You can't force them to be someone they're not.

'My oldest—he's a lot like you. Clever. I don't have a clue what he's talking about half the time, and he knows that. But I make sure he knows it doesn't mean I don't love him.'

'That's good.' Quinn paused. 'I always felt I was a burden to your parents. That they didn't really want me there.'

'We were a bit short on space—and money,' Sam admitted. 'But it wasn't your fault. And I don't think they meant to make you feel left out.'

'A lot of the time I felt as if they were angry with me.'

Sam shook his head. 'They weren't angry with you—it was your mum. And you were definitely better off with us than with her. I remember your mum,' Sam said. 'I don't mean to be rude, but she's probably the most self-centred person I've ever met. Even as a ten-year-old, I could tell that. When I was younger, she used to sweep in—you could smell her perfume half a mile away—and she expected Mum to wait on her hand and foot. And the way she just left you...' He shook his head. 'I don't understand her at all. I could never have done that with any of my three.'

So Carissa had been right about that. His

uncle and aunt hadn't seen him as a burden. They'd worried about him, cared—they just hadn't known how to tell him or show him. And, with a child's perspective on the situation, he hadn't been able to see that for himself. He'd just felt like an outsider.

'Mum and Dad tried to make up for her, but I guess you can't do that,' Sam continued. 'And maybe they didn't try hard enough, if you felt you were in the way. It wasn't fair on you.' He paused. 'And I know they feel bad that you had to bail us out three years ago.'

'What was I meant to do—leave you all to the mercy of the bankruptcy officer and watch everything you'd all worked for being taken away from you?' Quinn grimaced. 'Though I could've been more tactful about the way I did it.'

'Yeah. Dad's proud,' Sam said. 'It made him feel ashamed.'

'I guess I wanted to pay you all back for what you'd done for me. I wasn't trying to rub your noses in it and make you think that I was some kind of big shot. Because I'm not.'

'Quinn, you just moved to Belgravia. Of course you're a big shot,' Sam said, rolling his eyes. 'You've done well for yourself.'

Maybe, but he'd also missed out on a lot. Family things. He barely knew his family. 'I don't even know your kids. Just their names,' he admitted. 'Sending money for birthdays and Christmases—it isn't enough.'

'She must be really special,' Sam said softly, 'if she can make you see that.'

'She is.' Though he might have messed that up permanently, too. 'You can't change the past. I guess all you can do is learn from your mistakes and make things better for the future.'

'I'll drink to that.' Sam raised his coffee cup. 'It wasn't all your fault. We all made mistakes, too. I was the oldest. I should've made more of an effort.'

'You were ten years older than me. As a baby, I would've been a nuisance, taking your mum's attention, and when I started walking and talking you were a teenager—you weren't going to be interested in a toddler.'

'I still should've made more of an effort. We all should.'

'Maybe,' Quinn said, 'the new year can be a new beginning. It's not going to be easy, and I have a lot of bridges to build.'

Sam regarded him for a while. 'Yes, you do. But it's easier to build a bridge together than on your own. So if you want a hand building those bridges, maybe we can make a start.'

'I'd like that. And I'm sorry, Sam.'

'Me, too. But you're right. You can learn from your mistakes. Maybe we all need to learn to talk more. I know my wife's changed me. And your girl…' He paused expectantly.

'Carissa.'

'Carissa.' Sam nodded. 'She'll change you.'

Quinn thought she already had. 'Tell me about your kids,' Quinn said. 'Your wife. Catch me up on what I've missed.'

Sam grinned, and took his phone out of his pocket. 'When you're seriously bored of seeing photographs of the kids and the puppy, just remember you asked for it.'

Quinn smiled back. He'd definitely done the right thing.

At the end of the afternoon Quinn left his cousin, feeling decidedly better. And it was all thanks to Carissa pushing him into thinking about the situation properly and working out how to change it.

Could he fix the rest of it—the damage he'd done to himself and Carissa?

Because he knew now that he loved her. Not in the way he'd loved Tabitha—this was something that filled his soul. He'd fallen in love with Carissa Wylde. With a sweet, charming, lovely woman who loved playing fairy godmother and making other people's worlds a better place. OK, she could be a little bit bossy—but he liked that side of her, too. She was organised and determined, the kind of person you'd want on your team rather than the opposition. The kind of person who made things happen rather than just talking about it.

Accept yourself for who you are. Because if you can't do that, you'll never be able to really accept that someone can love you, and you won't be able to let yourself go enough to really love them back.

Could he accept himself for who he was?

A man.

One who made mistakes.

One who was great at his job but wasn't so good at the emotional stuff.

But he was prepared to try. To make the effort. To make things as right as he could.

Quinn thought about it.

And thought about it some more.

And he knew that he was really going to have to do something special to get Carissa to talk to him.

The supermarket was heaving with people doing a last-minute shop for party food, but he managed to get what he wanted—including something he thought Carissa might like. The one thing she hadn't included in her magic-of-Christmas proofs—but then again it wasn't really a Christmassy thing.

And he also needed her to know just how serious he was about this. Which meant doing something that scared the hell out of him but he thought it was the only way forward.

Half an hour on the internet found him exactly what he wanted.

And a phone call to the designer—plus some sweet-talking on his part—got him an out-of-hours appointment.

He knew the ring was the right one the moment he saw it. A narrow band of platinum with a heart-shaped diamond in the centre, in a sleek platinum setting. It was discreet and beautiful, like Carissa herself.

This was the biggest risk he'd ever taken in his life. A commitment. Actually letting someone get close to him. They could both end up very, very badly hurt.

Or they could both end up being really, really happy.

There was no middle ground. Double or quits. They'd played that game before, but this time it was for real.

He had to trust her. Trust *himself.*

'I'll take it,' he said, and had the ring placed in a navy velvet box, then wrapped in sparkly silver paper and tied with a navy chiffon ribbon.

CHAPTER FOURTEEN

IT WAS STARTING to snow when Quinn got back to the mews. He could see several lights on in Carissa's windows, so he was pretty sure she was home.

The question was whether she was alone, or whether—as it was New Year's Eve—she was throwing a party. Or going to one. Or…

He called her.

She didn't pick up.

And he didn't want to leave a message. He needed to talk to her. Face to face. Nothing else would do.

OK. He'd have to take a risk. If she turned him down, she turned him down.

It didn't take him long to set up the living room.

The picnic was in the fridge, along with the champagne and the most decadent chocolate cake in the history of the universe.

All he needed now was Carissa.

He rang her doorbell. There was no answer and he wondered if he'd missed her, but then he glanced at his watch. It was too early to go to a party.

He rang the doorbell again. There was still no answer; but he'd noticed movement in one of the lit rooms. She was there, then. Just not answering the door.

Well, he knew a little trick that might change that.

This time he leaned on the doorbell and didn't stop until she opened the door, looking annoyed. She clearly dressed for a party, in killer high heels and a little black dress; her hair was piled up on the top of her head and she was wearing a headband that he suspected had real gemstones rather than being a piece of costume jewellery.

'Oh—Quinn.' Her face shuttered.

Hardly surprising. He'd hurt her. He just wanted her to give him the chance to put it right. He'd thought about it. He'd accepted himself for who he was. And now he wanted the rest of his life—the rest of their lives—to start properly.

'I need to talk to you,' he said. 'I can see that you're going out, and I don't want to hold you up, but can you give me ten minutes? Please?'

She looked wary, and guilt flooded through

him. Given that her last relationship had been with a man who'd let her down, who'd hurt her physically and mentally, and whose apologies had always been short-lived, it was no wonder that she looked wary. Right now he needed to pull out all the stops. Make her see how he really felt. Make her believe in him and in their future.

'If you want me to go down on my knees and beg,' he said, 'I will.'

She looked shocked. 'Quinn, you can't do that. It's snowing!'

He shrugged, not caring about getting wet or cold. 'I'll do whatever it takes to make you realise I'm serious—that I really do mean it.'

For a nasty moment he thought she was going to say no.

But then she exhaled sharply. 'OK. Come in.'

'Um—I'd like to do this at my place.'

She frowned. 'What difference does it make where we talk?'

A huge difference. 'I know I don't deserve this, given that you had to ask me to leave,' he said, 'but would you humour me?'

There were shadows under his eyes. As if he'd slept badly, spent a lot of time thinking things through. Did this mean that he'd finally sorted out the demons in his head and he was ready to believe in himself—and in their future? Or was he going to tell her that he'd changed his mind?

Whatever happened, it was New Year's Eve. So whether it was closure or a new start, she'd get to start the New Year with a clean slate. The waiting would be over.

Much as she wanted to wrap her arms tightly round him and kiss him until they were both dizzy, now wasn't the time. They needed to talk.

'OK.' She grabbed her keys, locked the door behind her and followed Quinn to his house.

He paused in the hallway outside his living room. 'Wait here and close your eyes.'

What kind of game was he playing? 'Why?'

'Please—I'll only be a couple of seconds.'

She'd gone this far, so she might as well do what he asked. It wasn't going to make much difference. She closed her eyes. 'OK.'

He kept her waiting for more than a couple of seconds, but then she heard him come back into the hallway.

'Ready,' he said. 'You can open your eyes now. Come in.'

Carissa couldn't quite believe it when she walked into his living room. The austere, functional space she'd seen before had totally changed. Instead of the stark lighting Quinn normally used, there were tealight candles flickering on every surface, and rose petals were scattered everywhere; a soft cello concerto was playing in the background.

It was the most romantic thing she'd ever seen in her life.

And it was the last thing she'd expected from Quinn O'Neill.

'This is why I wanted you to come here. I wanted you to see that I'm serious,' he said. 'That I mean every word I say.'

'All this—it's beautiful—but…' She shook her head. 'It's just not you.'

'It's not me,' he agreed, 'but I thought you might like it—and I'm trying to make you feel some of the magic that you showed me.'

What?

Was she hearing things?

'Will you sit down?' he asked, gesturing to the sofa.

She sat down, and he sat next to her.

'You were right to throw me out,' he said. 'And I've had a lot of time to think this week.' He paused. 'I went to see my cousin today.'

Something else she hadn't expected him to say. 'And?' she asked carefully.

'You see things very clearly,' he said. 'You were right about everything. Sam's ten years older than me, so he was kind of a bit removed from it all. He said they were angry with my mum for dumping me, they didn't have a clue how to deal with me when I started being a maths geek, and talk of university worried them even more. All they could think about was student riots and people taking drugs, and they didn't want me to end up in trouble or get hurt.'

He smiled wryly. 'We've been at cross purposes for a lot of years. But Sam's got three kids. He sees things from a different perspective now. We can't ever change what happened, but we've made a start at getting things right in the future. It'll take time, but I'm going to see them again at the weekend. All of them.' He paused. 'You were right about that. And everything else, too.'

'Everything?' she checked.

'About learning to accept myself for who I am and see myself for who I am. I make mistakes and I bury myself in work so I don't have to face them. But this week I've faced a lot of things, and it feels as if the weight of half a world has fallen off my shoulders.' He held her gaze. 'And now I want the rest of my life to start properly, Carissa. I accept who I am. I'm ready to move on. And I've met someone who has taught me that there's good in life. Magic, even.'

She felt her eyes widen: did he mean her? Did he mean her failed attempts to prove the magic of Christmas to him?

Either she'd spoken aloud or it was written all over her face, because he smiled. 'Not Christmas,' he said, 'and I don't think I'm ever really going to like Christmas—even though Christmas this year was the most amazing day of my life. But this woman taught me that life can be magical with the right person. She taught me to look for the happy stuff. For the sparkle.'

So he *did* mean her.

He slid off the sofa and dropped to his knees in front of her.

'I want my future to be full of that magic,' he said. 'And hers. Because she's taught me that what I want is a family of my own. I might get it wrong every so often and need a bit of a nudge to get me back on track, but I'm going to try my best to get it right.

'I love you, Carissa Wylde. I love you more than I ever thought it was possible to love someone. It scares me stupid, but nothing can make me stop loving you. Ever. And I know you're about to go out and my timing's rubbish, but I'm going to ask you anyway. Would you do me the honour of marrying me and making a family with me?'

She couldn't quite take this in. 'You want me to marry you?'

He took a box from his pocket wrapped in sparkly silver paper and wrapped with a navy chiffon ribbon, and handed it to her.

The last time he'd given her a parcel wrapped in sparkly paper it had been star-shaped fairy lights for her computer screen.

But this box was much smaller.

'For me?' she checked.

'For you,' he said. 'I've never done this before. And I hope I'm doing this right.'

And he looked really, really nervous. Nervous enough for her to think she knew exactly what was in that box.

It took her three goes to untie the ribbon, partly because her hands were shaking and partly because it was really well tied.

Finally she undid it and took off the paper to reveal a navy velvet box.

She opened the box and just stared at the ring nestled within. It took her breath away: a heart-shaped diamond in a simple platinum setting. Simple and utterly beautiful. Quinn's heart, literally and figuratively.

She knew he was waiting for her to speak, but she couldn't get the words out.

His eyes were filled with anxiety. 'Did I get it wrong? Do you hate it? Because I can take it back if you hate it.' He swallowed hard. 'Or if you don't want it at all.'

How could he think that she wouldn't want what he was giving her? Because it wasn't just a ring. He was giving her *himself.* 'It's gorgeous and I love it. I'm just… Oh, Quinn…' She could feel tears trickling down her face and scrubbed the back of her hand against her skin to rub them away. 'You really mean this?'

'I really mean this,' he said.

She slid off the sofa to join him on her knees. 'Then, yes, Quinn, most definitely yes—I'll marry you. Because I love you, too, and I've been so miserable without you these last few days.'

'Me, too. But you were right to throw me out. I needed to work through the stuff in my head, and the only person who could do that was me. You showed me how to do it, but I had to sort it out for myself. Face up to who I am, and learn to believe that it's OK to let people close.'

'It's more than OK to let me close,' she said. 'Quinn O'Neill, you're everything I want.'

He held her so tightly that she almost couldn't breathe, but she was holding him just as tightly. Then he drew back slightly and gestured to the box. 'May I?'

She nodded and he took the ring from its velvet setting. He lifted her left hand, kissed the back of her ring finger, then placed the ring on it.

'I love you,' he said.

'I love you too.'

He gave her a rueful smile. 'I really haven't thought this through properly—I made you a picnic, all healthy stuff so you'd like it, and I put the rose petals and tealights where the food should go—and anyway you're supposed to be at a party.'

She smiled back. 'It's a casual thing, so it doesn't matter if I go or not, or if I take someone with me. We could go together, if you want to?'

'Right now,' he said, 'I'm selfish enough to want you all to myself and I don't want to share you with a crowd of strangers.'

'That works for me. I'll just text my friend so she doesn't worry.' She paused. 'Um, Quinn, you do know my family's going to want to celebrate this when we tell them the news? And that means a huge party with everyone there. Are you going to be OK with that?'

'I like your family,' he said.

'Just so you know, Gramps and Granny

liked you very much.' She smiled. 'And Poppy's already told me that you're a good 'un. Nan adores you. That's not going to change.'

'Good. And maybe you can come with me to Birmingham. Meet *my* family,' he said.

'I'd love to.'

He kissed her. 'You might need to nudge me every so often to get me back on track,' he said, 'but I'll try my hardest never to let you down again.' He paused. 'The last time I drank champagne with you,' he said, 'I let you down. Will you let me make that right?'

She nodded.

'Stay there and I'll bring the picnic in.' He grimaced. 'Well, maybe I'll clear things a bit first.'

'I like this room exactly as it is,' she said, 'candles and rose petals and all. It's the most romantic thing anyone's ever done for me— and I can't believe that someone like you, someone who hates mess and clutter and frivolous stuff, would do something like this.'

'For you, always.' He smiled. 'Give me two minutes.'

'Can I help bring anything in?'

'No.' He kissed her. 'Just stay there and text your friend.'

He came back a couple of minutes later with two glasses, a bottle of champagne and what looked like the richest chocolate cake in the world, topped with an enormous candle.

'I thought you said it was a healthy picnic?' she asked, laughing.

'Ah. That's still in the fridge. I'm cutting to the important stuff,' he said. 'Haven't you ever heard that you should eat dessert first?'

'That,' she said, 'sounds like an excuse for chocolate.'

'Not just chocolate. We should have fireworks as it's New Year's Eve, but it's freezing outside and it'll be heaving with people if we go to see the fireworks at the Thames—so this is my compromise, a private firework party.'

Knowing exactly what the candle was now, she grinned. 'A very private firework party.' One with an indoor Roman candle.

He opened the champagne and poured them both a glass, then lit the Roman candle and let it sparkle away.

'To you, Carissa,' he said, lifting his glass. 'Because that firework is how you make me feel all the time. I love you.'

'That's how you make me feel, too,' Carissa said. 'I love you.' The diamond in her engagement ring sparkled in the light from the fire-work. 'Always.'

'Always,' Quinn echoed, and kissed her.

* * * * *

LARGER-PRINT BOOKS!
GET 2 FREE LARGER-PRINT NOVELS PLUS
2 FREE GIFTS!

(H) HARLEQUIN®

Romance

From the Heart, For the Heart

THEY LOST THEMSELVES in a whole new world. There were wood-carvers, glassblowers and bakers. There were shoe-makers, cuckoo clocks and gingerbread. There was noise and life and vigor, and he watched as it brought Addie alive and filled her with delight. They stopped to watch a medieval dance troupe perform a folk dance, the scents from the nearby food stalls filling the air. When the dance was complete she took his arm and headed down a different alley. "This is amazing! Have you ever seen anything so amazing? It's just…"

His mouth hooked up. "Amazing?"

"Nutcrackers!"

He glanced from her face to the items she pointed to. An entire stall was devoted to small, and not-so-small, wooden soldiers.

"Colin would love these!" She selected four and paid for them all on her own, never once asking him to interpret for her. He shook his head. She definitely wasn't afraid of venturing forth on her own.

I want to be useful.

He had overcome that barrier now, hadn't he?

She oohed and aahed over chimney sweeps made from dried plums and almonds. She bought some gingerbread.

"Uh, Addie, I'm not sure you'll get that through Australian customs."

"Who said anything about posting this home? It's for us now." She opened the bag and broke off a piece. He thought she might melt on the spot when she tasted it. She held the bag out to him, and lunch suddenly seemed like hours ago. He helped himself to a slice. She grinned at whatever expression passed across his face. "Good, isn't it?"

He took some more. "Really good."

He bought them mugs of glühwein and they drank it, standing around one of the makeshift fires that dotted the square, Addie's holiday mood infecting him. He drank in the Christmas goodness and watched as she tried to choose a wooden figurine for Frank. "What do you think?" She turned, holding up two carvings for his inspection. "Father Time or the billy goat?"

He could tell by the way she surveyed the goat that it was her favorite. He didn't doubt for a moment that Frank would love either of them. "The goat."

He took her parcels from her so she could browse unencumbered. They stopped to watch a glassblower shape a perfect snowflake—an ornament for a Christmas tree—but he preferred to watch her.

When was the last time he'd relished something as much as Addie was relishing this outing?

Did you enjoy this sneak preview?
Don't miss the magical
SNOWBOUND SURPRISE FOR THE BILLIONAIRE
by Michelle Douglas, on sale December 2014—only
from Harlequin® Romance!